IN A SNOWDROP KISS

❄

ALEX GILLIE

TWENTY-FIVE DAYS UNTIL CHRISTMAS

❄

"*M*erry Christmas and thank you for supporting local," Holly said with a smile as she waved to Mrs. Barley who left the store with a bouquet in hand.

It was the first week of December and the magic *and money* of the Christmas season was in the air. The Town of Coal River twinkled with lights strung around the streets. Holly reached up to adjust the crystal snowflakes that hung in the shop windows.

She twirled the strands of her long blond hair around a flower-shaped pen from her apron pocket and fastened it tightly against her scalp.

"Another day done," Mia said, as she flipped over the hand-painted *Closed* sign and locked the flower shop door.

"Another customer happy," Holly replied, as she walked over to the counter and opened the register, pressed print on the digital point of sales machine, and started to count the bills for the day.

A knock sounded at the front door. Holly looked up to see her roommate, Rowena, tapping on the glass of the door and rubbing her arms. The weather had taken a turn for the worst this week with a cold snap coming in from the west. Mia quickly walked over and flicked the knob of the lock to let Ro inside.

"Why do we live somewhere that gets this cold?" Ro said as she hung her coat on a spare chair. Ro often came over at the end of the workday to wait for Holly to finish closing up her shop. Ro worked at the bakery just a few doors down and they would walk home together.

Holly's staff, Mia and Finley, didn't blink twice at the appearance of Rowena at the door. Mia grabbed the broom from the back closet and started to sweep up the fallen leaves and petals on the floor.

Holly scrunched her nose as she looked down at the numbers on her reconciliation sheet. She would have to input them into her budgeting software this weekend. The holiday season had been busy, but not busy enough. Local orders had held steady, but special events and large orders were becoming scarce.

She glared at the soggy spot in the ceiling that had been growing for the last few weeks. Holly had painted over it a few months prior when money was particularly tight, but the brown stain penetrated the creamy white ceiling paint within a few weeks.

Then a mushroom had grown out of it. A few customers had commented on it, making it difficult for her to ignore any longer.

"So, do you think you'll come?" Mia said, looking at Holly expectantly. She had missed the question.

"Sorry, I was miles away," Holly gave the girls an apologetic smile.

"Shawn and Simon invited us to drinks tonight." Ro jumped in, moving her pitch-black hair over her shoulder. She leaned back in the chair, leveling Holly with a look that was all too familiar. Ro was not only Holly's roommate, but she was also her confidante and unrelenting wingwoman. She was the Yin to her Yang. Tall where Holly was short. Stoic where Holly was bubbly. Hard where Holly was soft. Yet, they had been best friends for as long as Holly could remember.

"Can I come?" Finley asked before Holly could respond. He poked his head out from the storeroom.

"Sorry kid." Rowena patted him on his shoulder. "Adults only."

Finley frowned. "But I'm twenty-one," he mumbled under his breath as he disappeared behind the door. Returning with a watering can, he started to fill up the display cases, grumbling the whole time.

Mia gave him a sympathetic look. Finley was the youngest of the staff, only nineteen when he started working for Holly and he had been head over heels for Holly's roommate ever since. Not that Ro noticed or minded. She treated him like one of her kid brothers— of which she had three.

"Simon is the bartender with the cute bum from the pub. The one that was definitely flirting with you last week."

"I don't think he was," Holly said absentmindedly, stopping her count of the bills from the register. She swore she heard a drip somewhere. Great, now she lost count. She sighed and started counting again from the top as Mia recounted the last encounter with Simon and Shawn from the pub. Mia had been out with Shawn a few times already in the last week and Holly had heard in detail about each date in the quiet moments of the day.

Drinks would have been nice. Holly heard the drip again. She looked at the numbers on the reconciliation sheet and frowned again. She folded the paper and stuffed it in her apron pocket. She didn't want to worry the staff just before Christmas.

"Sorry guys, I am meeting Jack here for some repairs around the shop."

"You need to get out more, Holly, this shop is becoming your life." Rowena stuck out her bottom lip. Ro had been on Holly's case for months now. And to be fair, Holly had not been on a date in a while. Since Benji, and Holly didn't talk about Benji. To be honest, the shop was her life. It *had* to be her life. Especially with the piles of bills that had recently become so high she could practically call them a novel. The shop had thrived when her mother owned it. And she would not let it fail under her guardianship. She *couldn't* let it fail.

"I went out last weekend, didn't I?" Holly said absentmindedly.

Holly heard the drip again. Spending time on shop repairs was not an excuse. Well, maybe it was a little bit of an excuse, but she did have plans with Jack. And the shop needed attending to.

"Sorry," she said again, trying to look as sincerely apologetic as possible.

"Ugh," Mia exclaimed, putting the broom back in the closet with an exaggerated sigh. Ro stuck her hand out and Mia passed her a five dollar bill.

"I feel like I should be offended by that." Holly laughed.

"Well if Jack is coming over, tell him about the weird toilet flush. That thing hasn't been right for weeks."

Holly looked in the direction of the staff washroom and cursed internally.

"Sure, yeah, I'll let him know." Holly lied, with no intention of telling Jack about the toilet. She pulled her lips into a thin smile that she hoped rang true.

"Have you never thought about Jack?" Mia said, with a gleam in her eye.

"What about him?" Holly replied, narrowing her eyes. She knew when Mia got this look in her eye that nothing good would come of it. It was a mischievous look as if she had something planned. Ro looked at Mia with a look that said that she had asked this same question before and knew the answer.

"No," Holly said definitively, looking between them. "Never." But she felt the lie on her lips. Ro narrowed her eyes at her.

Holly busied herself with closing down the store computer system, trying to avoid her gaze.

There was a time at the end of high school when she thought maybe she and Jack could be *something* together. There were moments. Touches here and a prolonged gaze there. But they had both gone their separate ways during college and those feelings had fizzled out. Now they were just good friends.

"You guys head out. I'll finish up here. Jack is going to meet me here anyways," Holly said. Finley hung up his apron in the back shop, Ro nodded, and Mia grabbed their jackets.

"At the very least he has a cute butt too," Mia called out as she winked at Holly and the three left the store. Holly rolled her eyes as she locked the door behind them. She rested her head against the cool glass. She smiled a little as she heard Finley claim that he also had a cute butt. But the girls rebuffed him, saying his but was cute like a little Gerber baby bottom.

"Who has a cute butt?" A gruff voice said from the back of the store. Holly jumped. She had forgotten that she had given Jack a key to the back alley entrance.

Jack stood leaning at the back of the store wearing pale jeans and a plaid button-down that opened to a white t-shirt. His always scruffy blonde hair was tucked underneath a ballcap. An outfit that may as well be his own personal uniform. If Holly imagined Jack, this would be what he wore, or else it wouldn't be Jack.

Not that Holly ever imagined Jack.

Jack was just that– Jack. He had been a constant in Holly's life since before she could remember. Or at least since her mum started bringing her around the shop when she was a kid. He was the son of her mother's co-owner to the flower shop, Paulette.

Holly's mother, Margaret, and Paulette owned this shop for thirty years. Until Holly's mother got diagnosed with cancer and couldn't keep running the shop any longer. Paulette didn't have the heart to continue running the shop after she died. But Holly didn't have the heart to give it up.

"Uh, a guy we met at the bar… Simon? Yes... Simon." A lie.

Jack looked up at her and his brow furrowed for a fraction of a second.

She didn't know why she was lying. It was no secret that Mia thought that Jack was attractive. She had always teased that Jack was secretly a catch. He had that *small-town hotness* that apparently made him very appealing. According to her, he'd be the type of guy that would have no problem flinging you around in bed. In a good way.

But Holly did not dare to think about Jack in that way. It was a mental boundary that she didn't want to cross. But she did have to admit. Jack had only grown into his looks as he got older. She bit her lip, fiddling with a crochet flower on her sweater.

Holly couldn't tell what he was thinking. She felt her cheeks get hot.

"They invited us out for drinks." Holly blurted out before Jack could say anything. There was truth now in her lie. She wanted to fill the silence, lest her mind start to run away with thoughts of Jack and his cute butt.

"But I said I couldn't go. I had a date with you."

Jack paused. He gave her a look with his head cocked.

Shit.

"Well, not a date per se." Holly felt her heartbeat pound in her ears. What was happening? She was being weird. *Why was she being weird?* It was Jack.

Mia was getting in her head. She really was love-starved if she was thinking about Jack as a potential suitor. The boy that used to chase her around the store with slimy old flower stems and put pinecones in her chair when she wasn't looking.

Maybe Ro was right. Maybe she did need to get out into the dating world again.

"Not a date. An appointment." Holly tapped her finger on the wooden table as if to emphasize her point. His gaze followed her finger and Holly felt her heart quicken.

"I haven't been on a date in a while actually. No love life here, unfortunately." She resisted the urge to slap her forehead with the heel of her palm.

A small smirk started to form on Jack's face as if he could see the implosion happening in real time in her brain. Holly cursed internally.

"You mentioned a leak?" Jack finally spoke, changing the subject. Holly said a little prayer in her head, thankful for the intervention, which prevented her from further word vomiting about her dating life, or lack thereof.

"Ah, yes, up there." Holly pointed out to the spot on the ceiling. Jack looked up at the spot and his eyes went wide.

"Is that a mushroom?" Jack said, his mouth hanging open slightly.

Holly cringed. That was bad. Mushrooms were bad.

"Maybe?"

"I'll go grab my tools."

"Right," Holly said, nodding.

Jack left out the back and Holly mentally berated herself.

"How long has it been like this?" Jack asked, returning with a shiny red toolbox, the one Holly had given him for Christmas last year. Holly smiled. He had kept the forest green ribbon she had tied to the handle. Though to be fair, he had also kept all of the sale stickers on the box as well, but Holly liked to think it was because she was special in his heart.

"The leak? Uh, probably a week or so." Another lie. She was on a roll today. She didn't want to tell the truth that it had been there for a while and that she didn't have the funds to investigate it sooner.

"No, I meant your love life." He said with a crooked smirk, the same smile that had allowed the boy to get away with murder when they were young. *Great*. So she had been weird, and Jack had taken notice.

"Haha, you're very funny," Holly said as she gave him a hip bump and hopped up to sit on the counter while he grabbed the ladder from the back. He opened the frame in the store closet and entered the attic space through an access panel that was located there in the ceiling.

Holly leaned back and closed her eyes. A sigh escaped her lips before she could hold it in. It had been a long month. A long few years.

"You sure it's only been a week?" Jack called from the attic.

"Um, maybe a little longer," Holly replied, a sinking feeling settling into her stomach.

Jack finished in the attic and closed the hatch. He rubbed a hand behind his head. The sinking feeling grew.

"Hol, you're going to need to call an expert."

"I thought you were an expert," Holly replied, giving him a weak smile.

"A roofing expert." *Crap*.

"I can't tell exactly how much damage there is, or if it's

structural, but the wood up there has a lot of water damage. It looks like that leak has been there for a while. You may want to contract a structural engineer as well."

Crap. Crap. Crap.

Holly looked down at the sixty five dollars she had pulled out to pay Jack for his time. Even that amount of cash was tight for the shop. But a roofer and a structural engineer? She didn't have an idea of how much that would cost, but it sounded expensive. Very expensive.

Holly bit her lip. Hard. She would have to figure something out like she always did. She couldn't let her mom's store fall apart. Holly looked up at the cursed brown spot. Literally fall apart.

She folded the bills and rubbed them between her fingers, looking down at them. Holly could feel the corners of her eyes ache, the way they always did when she thought about her mom. She blinked, willing the feeling away.

"You ok, Hol?" Jack asked. His gaze softened.

Yes. Just say yes. Holly felt her face go red. Her eyes stung and she felt her chest get tight. She would *not* break down. Not now. Not in front of Jack.

Holly looked down and reached out, offering the bundle of bills to Jack.

"Here," she said. "For your time," Holly wasn't able to meet Jack's gaze for any longer.

Jack reached out, closing his hand around hers, folding the bills back into her palm. His hand was firm and warm around hers.

"I've told you before, you don't have to pay me."

"Just because you're a friend, doesn't mean you don't get paid for your time," Holly said stubbornly, pulling her lips together in a tight line. They had this conversation before. A million times before.

"How about you pay for pancakes," Jack said, another

crooked smile breaking through his stoic exterior. His head gestured in the direction of the pancake house just across the street. Jack and Holly had spent many a night in their youth there hanging out at that diner waiting for their moms to finish up work.

A grin broke out across Holly's face.

"You're on," she said.

"I've heard they are serving your favorite apple cinnamon snowman flapjacks."She winked at him. Jack rolled his eyes, but a small smile lingered on his face. They were, in fact, his favorite. And he would, in fact, be ordering them.

Jack waited for Holly to finish up closing, tinkering with the toilet flush Holly hadn't told him about. When she was done, Jack grabbed both of their coats, flipped the switch to the lights and held the door open for Holly as they exited the store. Holly took one look back at the now dark store and left the store with a sigh.

TWENTY-THREE DAYS UNTIL CHRISTMAS

❋

"Twenty five thousand dollars." Mia's mouth hung open exaggeratedly.

"That's what the roofers quoted us." Holly sighed, pinching the bridge of her nose between her forefinger and thumb.

"Well merry Christmas, I guess."

Holly thought the same. Christmas was a few weeks away and although everything around her reminded her of the upcoming festivities with twinkling splendor, she sure didn't feel like celebrating. What was supposed to have been her paycheck for the week went to paying a deposit for a structural engineer instead. And the man couldn't even come into the shop for another week. Apparently, the Christmas season was a busy season for everybody, engineers included.

"We need a Christmas miracle," Holly muttered under her breath as the phone rang. Holly picked it up.

"Bloom and Blossom Florist. Holly speaking, how can I help you?" Holly answered the phone in an identical greeting as every time she answered the phone. She could have been a robot at this point with how unchanged the tone was.

A woman spoke on the other end of the phone, asking if Margaret MacIntosh was in. Holly no longer cringed when this happened. It didn't matter that it had been three years since her mother had passed. Holly still received calls almost monthly from somebody asking for her mother.

Some of the clients were still interested in working with the shop under Holly. But Holly didn't have the awards that her mother had. She didn't have the reputation that her mother had.

Holly had only been in the business for a few years and although she was able to retain some of the clients on the coattails of her Mother's reputation. Holly just wasn't her mother.

Holly explained, in an identical way she did every time, that her mother had passed away and that she was now running the shop. The same awkward back and forth occurred where the client didn't know how to give condolences and exit the conversation. It sometimes ended with Holly having to comfort the client and listen to their memories of her mother or hear of a time that somebody they knew had cancer. Then the call would end. And the day would continue.

"No. No. Yes. She was a wonderful woman. I'm sure we can still help out with your event if you are still interested in using the Bloom and Blossom as a vendor."

Mia looked up from where she was assisting a customer, cocking her head so she could listen into Holly's conversation.

"Yes, excellent. I can set up a time next week to go over some details and get you a quote." Holly scribbled down the details of the client on the back of a used envelope and pinned it to the wall with one hand.

Holly gave Mia a thumbs up from across the room. It was

a small order, but a client conversion was a good thing. And they needed the money.

Holly gave a little happy dance, waving her hands in the air, before being admonished by Mrs. Greywell, who she was helping.

Holly hadn't kept the troubles away from Mia for the past few days. Especially with tradesmen in and out of the shop at all hours of the day. Holly tried to keep a smile on her face and her demeanor cheery to not let the disturbance interfere with the customer experience.

Naturally, word of the troubles at the Bloom and Blossom Florist soon spread fast in their small town. The shop had been busier than ever with busybody patrons. At the very least some of them bought some flowers while they were there snooping.

"It would just be such a shame if you had to close the shop." Mrs. Greywell said, clutching Holly's hands in hers. Her wrinkled hands were warm in Hollys. Holly cringed internally as the woman gripped her hands, refusing to let her hands go. Holly kept a pleasant smile on her face.

"This building has been in the town for over a hundred years. It's an important part of the town's heritage." Mrs. Greywell was a member of the town's Heritage Board, and when Holly had bought the shop, Mrs. Greywell had taken it upon herself to bring Holly in front of the board and provide her with a thorough education on the history of the building.

"You must promise to never sell it to one of those big investment agencies from the City." Mrs. Gladwell nodded in finality as if she were one of the decision-makers on what to do about the building.

"I'm not planning to sell the shop, Mrs. Greywell." The smile on Holly's face didn't quite reach her eyes. She *had* been approached by an investor in the summer, a Mr. Oliver Kilton. He was a charming man in a well-fitted suit. His company, the Ridgemont Investment Company, had bought out half of the stores on the main street in the past five years, renovating them into fancy storefronts. Glass and chrome and horrible LED lights, as Mrs. Greywell would complain.

The flower shop in comparison looked old, as old as it really was, quaint, but old.

The shop was built out of the old town saloon. Complete with a storeroom that still had the old double saloon door that swung open in the middle.

The card he had given her with the flash of a smile burned in her pocket. As did the pile of loan statements stacked on a bookshelf in her house. The flower store was a labor of love however.

Mrs. Gladwell gave her hands a squeeze and a pat.

"You're a good girl. Your mother did a great honor to this place, as will you, I'm sure of it," the woman said, giving her a dour look.

Holly said nothing back. She wasn't so sure she would be able to live up to her mother. In the eyes of the town, her mother was a saint. A single mother who raised her young daughter up right and who had dedicated herself to this town while she had lived. Holly's mouth went dry.

Mrs. Greywell gave her another squeeze before releasing her hands.

A bell rang and Holly looked up to see Jack enter the shop, through the front this time. Holly gave him a small wave.

Jack started to approach her before his eyes widened as he saw Mrs. Greywell. Jack did a sharp turn and pretended to be interested in a shelf of baby's breath as Holly rang up the older woman at the till.

"I see you there Mr. Stirling." Jack stiffened. He turned slowly feigning surprise at seeing Mrs. Greywell standing behind him.

"Oh, Miss. Greywell, I did not see you there." Jack said, putting his hands in his back pockets. Holly stifled a laugh and he shot her a look.

"You've been avoiding me." The woman tapped her shoe on the ground. "I haven't forgotten about those renovations that have been occurring in that cabin of yours. I would like the Cole River Heritage Board to take a look at the plans and approve any changes. That cabin is a point of interest, you know. It's very old."

"It was built in the fifties." Jack crossed his arms.

"Fifties, yes, that may be, but there has been a cabin in that spot since the eighteen hundreds. And history is history."

"Of course. I'll be sure to send those along," Jack mouthed, 'I won't be' to Holly as the woman searched her purse. "Here is my card. I do expect to be seeing them. And soon," She said, tapping her foot faster.

Another ring sounded at the door. Rowena entered the shop wearing a black minidress and matching tights. She wore a small black choker with a green Celtic knot dangling from the ribbon.

Mrs. Greywell narrowed her eyes at Rowena as she made her way towards Holly.

"Good god child. What in the devil made you go out in that on a day like today? You'll catch your death in clothes like that."

Rowena flicked the charm on her neck. "Don't worry Mrs. Greywell, it's the devil that is keeping me warm." She winked at the old woman, whose mouth hung open in shock. Mrs. Greywell took a step back, her eyes wide. Jack took the interruption to escape Mrs. Greywell's clutches.

"I think I hear somebody calling my name if you'll excuse me." Jack stepped to the side and disappeared into the back room of the store before the woman could say anything.

Mrs. Greywell let out a huff, her nostrils flared as she pulled her scarf around her closer and left the store.

"You're five. You shouldn't scare the patrons away." Holly rolled her eyes at Ro.

"What, it could have been the devil, or it could have been my fleece-lined leggings. Plus, I'm pretty sure her ancestors burned mine in the seventeen hundreds." Ro shrugged.

"Yes, well witch-hunter or not, Mrs. Greywell still buys a bunch of flowers nearly every other week and I need her patronage." Holly rubbed her fingers against her thumb.

"What if you do a fundraiser?" Ro said, spinning around, "I could sell my famous gooey chocolate chip cookies. I could ask the bakery if they would let me use the kitchen for a weekend."

"A cookie fundraiser for twenty-five thousand dollars?" Jack's sarcastic voice rang out from the back of the shop where he was tinkering with a shelf that had become rickety.

"Why are you here again?" Ro asked Jack.

"I'm working," he said, waving a wrench around. "Why are you here? Did the people at the graveyard finally ask you to leave?"

Ro shot him a glare.

Holly sighed. She let her shoulders slump and sat back in the chair at the till.

"Maybe it's worth a shot," She said, covering her face with hands so she couldn't see the look Jack was giving her.

"People do love cookies at Christmas time." Ro slid a chair in between Holly and Jack so that her back was facing Jack.

"This is a flower shop, not a cookie shop," Jack deadpanned. Ro turned around and scowled at Jack. Jack wasn't wrong, but the extra cash would help. *Any* little penny would help.

"I'll make flower-shaped cookies," Ro said, ignoring Jack's quips.

"We *could* sell them with Christmas mini bouquets." Holly ran her fingers down her face, making the reds of her eyes show.

"I don't think you should be worried about me scaring away patrons with a beautiful face like that. Very attractive look." Ro stuck her tongue out between her teeth and Holly threw her flower pen at her.

"You know Simon is working at the Christmas fair this year as their marketing specialist. I'm sure he could swing a table for us if we asked really nicely." Mia chimed in, with a pair of shears in hand.

"I thought Simon worked at the pub?" Holly cocked her head.

"He's the marketing manager for the pub." Mia grinned, putting the sheers down and leaning on the back of the chair that Ro was sitting on. From that angle she was giving Jack a good view of her backside, had he been looking.

"He's doing the Christmas market as a favor to the town. Which you would have known, had you shown up at drinks the other night." Mia leveled her with a look as if she was a naughty child who hadn't done her homework.

"You know I'm your boss, right?" Holly asked with a laugh.

Mia waved Holly off. They both knew they treaded a thin line between employee, boss and friends. Mia was only a year younger than Holly and she had joined the shop when she had moved to Cole River. She had never revealed to Holly why she had moved to the small town, and had come with no connections. No friends or family in the area. They became fast friends, and Holly had never pressured Mia to tell her. She wasn't sure if Mia was running away from something or towards it. She figured that Mia would tell her if the time was right. What Holly did know, however, was that Mia was overqualified for her position at the shop, and she was happy to have Mia working at the shop for as long as she wanted to. She was an excellent employee.

"Maybe I need to set up a date between you and Simon." Mia winked at Holly, pushing the boundaries between friend and employee.

"What does a pub need marketing for?" Jack frowned.

"Maybe I could meet with him." Holly opened up a notebook, scribbling out some ideas for bouquet designs. The Christmas market was a huge event in town and notoriously difficult to get a table in. It was one of the major tourist attractions that brought in even a bunch of people from the neighboring cities, to get a taste of pretend small-town life, *a la Marie Antoinette*. It would be an excellent opportunity for some sales and would expose them to clients outside their small town.

"You should wear that cute little black dress that you wore for your birthday," Mia said, a glint twinkling in her eye.

❄

"I'm telling you. Every time I do a reading for you there are good signs for love this year." Holly and Ro were on the floor of their living room. They were seated on a plethora of half-falling-apart cushions that Holly had patched with embroidery over the years. Rowena claimed that sitting on the floor helped ground you to the earth and Holly learned to not argue years ago.

Holly and Rowena lived in her mother's house. It was a quaint old foursquare that had way too many bedrooms and way too many floorboards that squeaked when you walked on them. Like most of the houses in this part of town, the old part, the house was built a few centuries ago and the age was showing. But Holly wouldn't have it any other way.

Rowena shuffled the cards and then placed two next to each other on the table. The first card Ro flipped over had two figures, a man and a woman, each holding a golden chalice. This was one of their nightly rituals after work. Rowena and Holly would make dinner and spend the evenings on the floor of the living room, eating, chatting, and sometimes telling fortunes.

"The two cups," Ro explained, tracing her hands over the face of the card. "This card is about partnership. Connection. A union to be reckoned with."

"Maybe it's talking about you and me?" Holly teased, grabbing one of the sugar cookies they had made this afternoon and popping it in her mouth. She had already eaten about five this evening and her teeth were starting to hurt.

"I don't think so," Ro said. She flipped over the second card so that it was facing Holly. The card was of a beautiful woman, sitting confidently on a throne and holding a long golden staff.

"This is the Queen of Wands. She usually is associated with passion. And when paired with the Two of Cups, it's usually of a sexual nature. And as much as I love you with all of my heart, I don't think we'd work out." Ro waggled her eyebrows and then gave Holly a kiss on the cheek.

"I thought we were going to be old maids together." Holly stuck her tongue out at Ro. "Read it again."

As much as the people in the town joked about Rowena's family being the town witches, it was partially true. And Holly didn't mind. She got the benefit of being the best friend of somebody who would give her a tarot reading whenever she wanted it. And she made excellent creams and poultices for every and any type of ailment.

"Fine. But I am convinced that you're going to find your great love this year."

TWENTY-TWO DAYS UNTIL CHRISTMAS

❄

*H*olly buzzed, fidgeting with a loose button on the red knit dress she chose to wear. She had tried on the cute little black dress that Mia had recommended, but the tight fitting garb felt like she was trying too hard. Though Mia's advice to flirt did ring in her head, she wanted this to be more of a business transaction and not like she was using the poor guy for a date. She had morals, after all. Right?

Mia had changed it from a coffee date, then to a lunch, and now it was dinner. It was at the local diner, which wasn't exactly a fancy restaurant, so Holly reluctantly agreed.

She *needed* this table at the Christmas fair. Holly had run the numbers and if she could sell even half of her stock, she should be able to cover the cost of the repair. Her heart beat in her chest.

"Do you need a water refill?" The waitress asked, her thinly drawn eyebrows scrunched up in the middle. The waitress had a pitying look on her face like she knew Holly was nervous.

Holly had downed the glass of water in the first five

minutes she had been seated. Her mouth was parched in a way that the water didn't seem to moisten.

"Yes. Please."

"Sure thing, darling." The waitress said in the way that all waitresses in small towns did. She moved to pick up the extra menu from the table.

"Oh no, I'm still expecting someone." Holly smiled, patting the table.

"Oh. Of course." The waitress gave her a thin lipped smile.

Holly tapped the table a few times before double-checking the folder of information she had placed next to her. She grabbed a pretzel and popped it into her mouth. It gave a satisfying crunch as she bit into it.

Holly checked the time on her phone. 15 minutes late. He was *still* coming. She was sure of it, but she didn't even have his number to text him. Mia had set everything up. Five more minutes. She would give him five more minutes. Maybe ten.

Holly sat back, her shoulders deflated. This was officially a new low point. Was this payback for skipping on drinks the other night? Well, if it was, she didn't want to have his help anyway. What kind of person would be so cruel? Especially on Christmas. She slouched further in the booth. She felt like every eye in the diner was on her. The pathetic girl who had been stood up. Not that this was technically a date, but nobody else knew that. Just her and her date. Non-date date.

This was supposed to be the solution to all of her problems. Or at least her roofing problems.

Holly fiddled with her phone, going from app to app, trying to distract her from the sad circumstances she found herself in, and yet, she couldn't muster the will to leave. Holly pinched her nose and took in a deep breath. She counted the seconds on the clock. Each time the bell of the front door rang, her gaze was ripped up from her phone. Yet, each time, she was also disappointed.

As the seconds and minutes ticked by, the sting of rejection felt more and more palpable. Though this totally was not a date, so she willed herself not to feel hurt. Her stomach rumbled in protest at the late meal. She would wait a few more minutes. Maybe she would even order something to eat, as to not feel so pathetic just waiting here. She couldn't give up this opportunity.

Not quite yet. Not while there was still a glimmer of hope that Simon showed up. It was entirely possible that he was late, or maybe he had gone to the diner on the other side of town and had to run across town to get to the correct one.

Holly landed on the contacts app, reviewing and deleting old contacts of which she no longer remembered who they were. She had gone through A to O when her finger hovered over on the delete button for Oliver Kilton, the developer.

Holly couldn't remember putting his contact in her phone, and yet here he was, his contact staring right back at her. A mere click away.

'Coffee,' is what he said. No pressure to sign. No pressure to sell. Just to hear him out. To talk. What would it hurt to just talk?

Holly bit her lip. To sell would be defeat. But, having the shop to her own, especially without the guidance of her mother had been a lot to bear. More pressure than she had been expecting.

The bell rang again and she looked up. Maybe?

A chorus of laughter broke out as a large group of men walked into the diner as if the universe was mocking her situation. They were all wearing community hockey jerseys.

Right. It was Thursday— Hockey night.

She felt herself click the message button under Oliver's contact, her thumb moving as if on its own accord.

Her fingers froze over the keyboard and she chewed on her lip.

```
(H) Coffee. You mentioned
coffee. Still not selling.
```

Her heart beat in her chest as she heard the sent text swoop. She sat for a moment. Staring at the text message. Willing a response.

Her heart stopped. Three dots. He had read it and was responding.

Holly clutched her phone. Her finger tips turned white from the pressure.

"Holly?" a man's voice broke the silence of her mind. Her head shot up.

Jack stood at the end of her table, wearing a plain white tee under a navy sports jacket. The local hockey team's logo on the right breast. He was a part of the team. She knew this. He had mentioned it before.

And now he was here, a witness to her humiliation. Her low point. She felt her cheeks get hot as he looked down to the empty but set seat across from her and the empty snack bowl in the middle of the table.

Without a word, and without mentioning the clear signs that she had been stood up, Jack sat down.

"You don't have to keep me company," Holly said, looking down. "I don't want to bother your night with your teammates."

"They've barely noticed I'm absent," Jack matter-of-factly, nodding over his shoulder at the group of men who were jovially laughing at the table across the diner. It was true, none of them had glanced their way or noticed Jack was sitting with her and not them.

"It's the same every week," Jack said.

"Mark," he gestured to a stout man, with jet-black hair

that had wisps of silver in it, "is the captain and always orders way too much for the table."

"Lewis," he nodded to a wisp of a man with bright yellow hair, "always starts a fight with Frank, and then they don't speak for a week. Until the next game where they're then best buds again, then the cycle starts again." The man in question was talking very loudly with another teammate with a large nose and bright red cheeks.

He continued, describing many of his teammates and their particular idiosyncrasies. She knew he was just doing this to get her to relax, to take her mind off the fact that she had been sitting here alone and embarrassed. She looked over his face. She had never realized how observant he was.

Jack had certainly matured from the boy she grew up with. He was still a bit of a devil when he wanted to be, but he had a seriousness about him now. Through it all, there was still that streak of consideration for others that had always drawn her to him. She looked over his face. Light wrinkles had started to settle in the areas where he smiled.

He landed on the final teammate.

"And Tom over there with the red hair will drink a little too much and hit on the waitress with the blond hair." Holly looked back over to the table of loud men. Tom indeed had a large glass of beer in his hand and was looking at the blond waitress. The waitress herself seemed to glance over with a small smile every once in a while.

"He's working up the courage to ask her out one of these days."

Jack met her gaze. Her eyes flicked from one eye to the other. She had never noticed how dark his eyes were, like the sky before a big thunderstorm. Holly's heart quickened and she sucked in a breath. The world went still for a moment, the noise of the diner quieted around them, and it felt like they were kids again, hanging out, just the two of them, in the quiet moments of the early evening in the back of the shop, waiting for their mothers to finish the day. But something was different now and Holly could not quite put her finger on it.

Jack frowned as they held each other's gaze.

"What's stopping him?" Holly asked, her mouth going dry.

Jack paused, his face becoming serious. He took a deep breath in and held it. She could have sworn his eyes flicked down to her lips.

"I don't know." He responded. He looked lost as his brow furrowed. He broke her gaze, looking down. "Or maybe he's just afraid she'll say no and it'll ruin the good thing they have going for them."

"She won't say no," Holly said after a moment.

"How do you know?" He asked, looking back* at her intently.

"You can tell she's into him too," she said resolutely. She took a breath. She looked over to Tom and the waitress sitting together at the bar. Tom had worked up the courage to walk over to her. He had just said something funny as the waitress was looking at him with a shy smile that she was trying, and failing, to suppress.

His expression was unreadable. Jack swallowed. They sat there for a moment, looking into each other's eyes. He was so familiar to her. They saw or talked to each other almost every single week. But she had never seen this look in his eye before. Her breathing quickened as she swore he leaned in. Jack opened his mouth as the waitress came back.

"Oh good." She said with a warm smile. "Your date has arrived. I was getting worried there for you honey."

"Oh. No," said Holly, shaking her head. "Jack is just a friend. I'm still waiting."

The waitress made an 'oh' sound. For a second, Holly could have sworn Jack tensed.

The front bell rang again and a man with a mop of dark brown hair emerged from the street.

Simon.

❄

Holly breathed out a sigh of relief, but she couldn't help feeling a pang of loss. Loss of the moment that she and Jack were having.

Simon scanned the restaurant, before making eye contact with her and jaunting over.

"You're late," Holly deadpaned. She glanced at her watch.

"An hour late."

"I am," Simon said, not arguing. He brought a hand up to rub the back of his neck and gave her an apologetic, yet charming smile. He was the kind of guy that could get away with murder in this town. He was dressed in a casual baby blue button-down shirt with one too many buttons undone so you could see the hint of chest hair poking through and a pair of well-tailored tan trousers. He looked good and he knew it.

"I have no excuses other than work ran late." He flashed another charming smile.

"Will you forgive me?"

Holly thought for a moment. Glancing over at Jack, he watched the interaction with an unreadable expression. The hour didn't feel like an hour with his company. And she found herself wanting desperately to say no.

"Yes." She finally said. Simon brought his hands together in a prayer.

"Thank you," Simon said to Jack, pulling out one of the seats, "for keeping my girl company while she waited for me."

Holly could have sworn she saw Jack's eyebrow twitch.

"I wouldn't have needed to if you had been on time." Jack

leveled him with a look, making it clear that although Holly had forgiven him, he had not.

"Right, well as I said, work."

Jack stared at him, not saying a word.

"What's your problem, man?" Simon leaned back in his chair. Bringing an arm to drape over to the back of Holly's chair. Jack glanced at his arm for a split second, narrowing his eyes. His jaw flexed.

Simon noted the look, retreating his arm for a second. *What was Jack doing?* He was going to completely mess this up with his misplaced sense of gentlemenly-*ness*.

"Or am I missing something?" Simon looked between Holly and Jack in confusion.

"Mia said that you were single. Am I mistaken, and are you and this guy—" He trailed off for a second, looking between Jack and Holly.

"No. Definitely not" Holly said, probably a little too quickly.

Jack shot a look at her, and she felt a pang of regret. She was thankful for Jack, for keeping her company. But Simon had struck a nerve with Jack and she couldn't have him compromising the deal. She was angry for being snubbed, but she could deal with that herself.

"Jack, thank you for keeping me company. I can take it from here." She said. A moment of hurt flashed over his face before he schooled his face back to an impassive expression. Jack searched her eyes for a moment before nodding.

"Right." He said. Jack turned without another word and joined his teammates.

"Jack," Holly called after him, but he didn't turn around again.

There was a roar of cheering as Jack sat down at their table. One or two of his teammates threw a glance her way.

"So, Mia mentioned that you own a flower shop."

Holly's head whipped back to the man sitting beside her. He had a lazy smile on his face as he waved over the waitress.

"Yes," Holly said, composing herself. She was here for business. The moment with Jack could wait to be analyzed later. Likely in the wee hours of the night as she tossed and turned on her bed. That was, after all, when she did her best obsessing.

"Yes, I own the Bloom and Blossom Florists. The little one on Seventh Street, in the town centre."

Simon scratched his chin for a moment.

"Ah, yes, I know the one. I think I bought flowers there for mothers day this year. You've got a great spot there."

They settled into a casual conversation as the waitress came back over to grab their orders. Holly's shoulders relaxed. Simon was an easy conversationalist. She had remembered that from the pub, though she had a few more drinks than usual that night.

The food came out hot. He was casual and a little flirty as they ate their meal. Which, surprisingly, Holly didn't mind. It had been months since she had been properly flirted with, and even longer since she had been on a date. Not that this was a date. It was a business dinner. Yes, strictly business. And yet Holly hadn't quite gotten a chance to bring up the topic of the Christmas Fair.

"So–"

"So–"

They both spoke at once. Simon laughed as Holly gave a small smile.

"You go first," Holly said, looking at her plate. She took a deep breath, thankful for the little bit of extra time before she had to give her pitch.

"I would like to see you again." Holly's head shot up. He looked at her hopefully, and for the first time that night, he looked to be the nervous one.

"Again?" She said slowly.

But this wasn't a date. She didn't *want* this to be a date. Only a business meeting. Holly fiddled with her skirt in her hands. She snuck a glance over at the table Jack was sitting at, and she could have sworn he had been looking this way for a split second before she had looked over. Now, however, he was back to his conversation with the waitress who had been so kind to her earlier. The waitress was laughing at something funny Jack had said. Jack *was* funny. She had always seen it, but not many others in town got to see it. He was usually quiet, stoic and reserved around those he didn't know well.

Then Jack smiled, and a little piece of her heart crumbled. She sucked in a breath, feeling her cheeks go cold. It was the dazzling smile that Holly thought Jack had reserved for the quiet moments of the day when the two of them were alone. It was the smile she had always, selfishly and likely ridiculously, thought was reserved for her.

She didn't know why she felt so disappointed. Had she imagined the moment between the two of them earlier? She was so clearly starved for male attention that she started to fantasize that maybe Jack was interested in her. That there was something between them. Holly berated herself.

Jack had never brought a girl around her before. She knew that he had dated before. He had heard their names over the years, but he had always kept that part of his life separate from her. She didn't know why she was so... disappointed to be wrong.

Holly glanced back at Simon. He was looking at her expectantly.

"I think I should have gone first."

"Oh," he said. "That doesn't sound like a yes."

"Well, this isn't a date," she said.

"It's not?" Simon looked confused.

"No, it's a business meeting," Holly said. Simon raised an eyebrow and chuckled as Holly brought out a small black folder she had been preparing all week.

"I wanted to discuss the Christmas Fair with you." Holly could feel the adrenaline rising in her and she willed her hands and voice not to shake.

"The Christmas Fair?" Simon repeated.

"Yes," she said as she opened the folder and took a deep breath. She could do this.

"We wouldn't need a large table, just a small one. And as we are a late entry, I know that we won't be able to get one of the tables in the main part of the show, so we are very okay with getting a table in the perimeter, in one of the less desirable locations. Not that we could really afford the fees for one of the main tables. I took a look at the website, and I have here a company blurb, image in both digital and print, and some information on what we would be selling." Holly flipped through the folder, pointing out each sheet. Her heart raced as she felt herself start to ramble on about each of the floral bouquets and accompanying cookies that they would provide.

"So yes, we're really excited about this opportunity." Holly finally looked up with a big smile at Simon, and her heart sank.

Simon, who had been silent through her pitch, was frowning. Had she done too much, gone too hard. Was this not what was required? Holly looked back down at her folder and bit her lip. She had studied the requirements on the *Frequently Asked Questions* page of the Christmas Fair website. She had the little jingle that played on the website almost seared into her brain. If she heard the tune of *Jingle all the Way* one more time, she swore that she would scream.

"What?" She asked, bringing her hands to her lap, she wrung her dress between her hands.

Simon was silent for a moment as if considering his next words.

"Did Mia tell you that I could guarantee you a spot at the Christmas Fair?" He spoke slowly, and Holly got the sense that Simon would have used this tone of voice when telling a toddler that they could *not,* in fact, have another Christmas cookie, and that it was time for bed. Holly sucked in a breath.

Yes. She almost said.

She knit her brow together, recounting the conversations that she and Mia had over the past day about the not-date with Simon and the Christmas Fair. Mia had definitely said that Simon could get them a spot.

Or did she?

Had Holly imagined it.

A chill of horror fell over her as if somebody had put a cold blanket over her shoulders.

Mia had said that Simon could *possibly* get them a spot and that he had connections with the organizers. Holly had taken that as it was *very possible*, easy even, for Simon to make it happen. But now looking at Simon, and the gentle look he was giving her, Holly had the distinct feeling that she had taken it the wrong way.

"I'm so sorry," Holly blurted out, snapping the folder closed. She felt a fierce hotness grow over her ears and cheeks.

She stood.

The urge serged to bolt out the door and hide in her childhood closet, just like she did when there was a big thunderstorm when she was little. She had never missed her mother more.

A fool. A complete and utter fool is what she was at that moment. From the look on Simon's face, he knew it too.

"Please stay," Simon said gently, placing a hand on hers. Holly hesitated.

He was a kind man. She could tell that right away. He didn't make note of her foolishness, or berate her for her naive assumptions.

"At least stay for a slice of gingerbread pie. And tell me about your shop," he said, patting the black folder on the table.

Holly thought for a moment. She wanted the world to swallow her up. She glanced over to where Jack had been chatting with the nice waitress. But sometime during her not-but-maybe date with Simon, Jack had left. Holly chewed her lip.

With all hope lost, with every chance at salvation dashed, at least there could be pie.

TWENTY DAYS UNTIL
CHRISTMAS

❆

*H*olly hadn't seen or heard from Jack in two days.

She couldn't get the moment with Jack out of her head. Replaying it over and over. Had he been about to kiss her, or was it all in her head? She felt her heart flutter as she imagined how his eyes flick down to her lips, leaning in with his blue eyes. Her heart pounded in her chest. She felt like a teenage girl again who had found a note written to her by her crush in her locker.

What *would* it be like to kiss Jack? She brought up a hand unconsciously to her lips, pressing the tips of her fingers against her bottom lip. Maybe Ro was right. Maybe it had been too long since she had been laid.

"That good, huh?"

Holly's head snapped up, whipping her hand away from her mouth.

"What?"

"Your date second with Simon," Mia said as she leaned her forearms on the counter.

"Oh. Yeah, it went well." Holly blushed before she walked

over to one of the displays in the shop window and started to fiddle with how the red carnations fell over juniper stems in the hanging vases. She pulled and replaced them a few times. *Simon.* She should be thinking about Simon. The guy who had shown an active interest in her and not her childhood friend.

Simon. Simon. Simon.

She recited his name in her head. She would not think about Jack.

Holly had agreed to see Simon again for a proper date. He had taken them skating at the rink that was set up in front of Town Hall. Town Hall was decorated to the nines for the Christmas season.

Every year the town opened a large skating rink in front of the hall and erected a twenty-foot-tall Christmas tree in a tree lighting ceremony. They had food and drink stands, trinket vendors, and fire pits to roast marshmallows. It was a picturesque place filled with holiday cheer. A perfect spot for a date.

He didn't know that Holly hated skating. She had proceeded to fall several times before he suggested they stop for hot chocolate and churros at the food vendor stands. She had readily agreed.

Holly rolled a kink out of her neck.

They had a generally good time. Simon was an easy man to like. He was an easy conversationalist. They talked about their love for the town, their interests, and the shop. She told him about their roofing problems and the historic nature of the building. Simon was currently renovating a century home, so he sympathized with her on the many issues that came with a historic building, including having to deal with the Historic Board.

Holly stayed away from the topic of her mom. She wasn't quite ready to divulge that part of her heart to him yet.

Holly finished fiddling with the display and flipped the switch to the twinkle lights that lit around the flowers in the shop window. She placed a few scrolls of cinnamon in the bouquets and blew out the candle she had lit. The air smelled of a mixture of Christmas spices and florals in a way that made warm nostalgia fall over Holly.

Holly liked Simon. He was nice in a genial kind of way. He didn't think her pursuit of saving her shop was silly or stupid. He mostly talked about himself, if she was totally honest. Not in a bad way, Holly didn't mind listening to others. She was good at that. Good at being a good listener. Her mom had always told her that. However she had this nagging feeling like it wasn't right. That they weren't right.

She looked back at Mia as the clock on the wall chimed eight times, indicating the start of the day. Mia nodded back as if to say *we're ready*. Holly walked over to the shop door, flipped over the *OPEN* sign, and unlocked the door.

Customers filtered in throughout the day, picking up bouquets and florals for their Christmas parties, and holiday celebrations.

Holly still hadn't seen or heard from Jack.

❄

Holly tapped her fingers on the wooden table several times. She stared at the computer screen. Her business bank account was pulled up. She let out a guttural sound and then a scream. The store was closed and she knew nobody could hear her through the thick wooden walls. She dragged her fingers over her face.

The budget was thinning. Thick enough that she could still manage day to day operations, and pay her staff, but not thick enough to pay for any extras. She had even been skimming off her own pay these last few months.

She heaved a breath trying desperately to compose herself. To get her rampant emotions in check. Holly looked over the numbers again.

She had tried to call her bank for another loan, but they had essentially laughed in her face. She let out a big sigh. She knew what she had to do. But it was a last resort type thing. A thing that caused every fiber in her being to scream at her saying no.

Holly opened her phone and hit call.

The phone rang for a moment and a little part of her hoped that her father wouldn't pick up. A click sounded and a man's voice answered.

"Herschel MacIntosh speaking."

"Hi Dad, it's Holly."

"Holly?" Her dad sounded surprised. It had been a few months since she had spoken to him.

"I was just wondering if I could talk for a second. It's about the shop." She wanted to get to the point. This was humiliating enough to have to ask her father for money. Holly and her father had a strained relationship.

"You want money," he said flatly. Holly opened and closed her mouth several times. Yes. She wanted to cry. Yes. She needed money. She was desperate for money.

"You know I told you that it was a mistake to buy that place when your mother had died. It was never very profitable. You should have gone into finance like I told you." Holly had heard this many times before.

"No, Dad, I'm not asking for money." Holly lied. She had called to ask for money. But she couldn't listen to her father berate her.

"The shop is doing fine. We're very profitable. We're doing renovations and I was wondering if you remembered the last time the washroom had been renovated." It was a weak lie and she knew it.

"The washroom," he said slowly. "No. I don't remember when it was last renovated."

"Okay. That was it, thanks." She quickly closed the phone. Holly slid down the wall. She let out another groan. Her pride would not let her take money from that man.

❄

Holly knocked on the twin doors. The arched doors were a dark oak, carved with florals and celtic knots. In the summer months, vines of ivy cascaded up the brick walls of the two storey house. The Stirling home felt like it was out of a fairy tale. Holly felt at home here. She had spent just as much time here as a child as she had at her own home. She had found herself here without meaning to end up here.

Paulette opened the door, a warm smile spreading over her face as she saw Holly. Paulette was a small woman, though you wouldn't notice it from interacting with her. Her personality made her seem six feet tall and larger than an ox. She wore layers of long cardigans, scarves and shawls, with several layers of warm woolen skirts. Holly was sure her style hadn't changed since the seventies.

"Darling, I didn't know you were going to visit." A warmness fell over Holly, and her face began to crumple.

The smile was immediately wiped from Paulette's face and a look of concern replaced it.

"Oh, Holly." She said embracing Holly and bringing her arms around her.

Holly brought her hands to her face, letting herself feel vulnerable in the arms of the woman who had practically been her second mother. Paulette was possibly the only other person alive who might understand the stress that she was going through. Holly collected herself, releasing the embrace.

"Come inside darling and I'll make us a pot of tea,"

Paulette said, leading Holly into the house. Paulette's house was the definition of calm and cozy. Pictures of family and friends lined the moss green walls, along with knick-knacks Paulette and her husband, Ralph, had gathered on their travels. The house was decorated with candles and multi-colored Christmas lights, and the house smelled of freshly baked gingerbread cookies. Holly felt truly safe and warm here like she could finally relax.

Paulette led Holly to the kitchen, motioning for her to sit in the brown leather chairs at the kitchen island.

"Now, tell me what's going on, Hol," Paulette said, whisking around the kitchen to pull out a kettle from the cupboard. The burner on the range clicked three times before a flame sprang out from the element, engulfing the bottom of the kettle in a small ring of fire. She brought out two small tea cups decorated in blue and white flowers and put one in front of each of them, along with a small plate of shortbread.

"It's all a mess," Holly said, pinching her nose between her forefinger and her thumb as the kettle started to ring. Paulette walked over to the kettle and poured the heated water over the steeper which she had filled with a cinnamon and orange blend of tea leaf. Without asking, she plopped two cubes of sugar and a splash of milk into Holly's cup, just the way she liked it.

"It sounds like you're putting a lot of pressure on yourself," Paulette said, not asking what *it* was.

"I just don't want to disappoint everyone. You. The town. Mom." She sucked in a breath, taking a sip of the tea and letting the warmth run down her throat and fill her chest. She savored the feeling for a moment.

"Oh Hol, you would never be a disappointment to your mom. You were the light of her life."

Holly stayed silent for a moment. She knew that her

mother had loved her, but she couldn't help but feel like a failure. She wanted to wallow. She was so confused at the moment. She didn't know how to get out of the financial hole that was the shop. She bit her lip.

There was the roof, but there were also the other bills and debts. When she bought the shop she had assumed some of the debts that had accumulated when Paulette and her mom were running the shop, particularly during the year that her mom was sick. The last year of her life.

Holly never blamed Paulette or her mom for the debts. She bought the business knowing full well they existed. But in the past three years, the accruing interest on the debts had been creeping up. They had been made at the height of interest rates and the banks were keen to get their profit from them. Holly had been able to pay a few of them off when she first bought the store, with the excitement of a new owner bringing in excitement to the town and business into the shop, but not all of them.

And then there was Jack. Holly took another sip. She couldn't tell Paulette about Jack. How she was feeling confused about how she felt about him. *If* she even felt something for him. If he felt maybe something for her.

Just as she opened her mouth, she heard the keys to the door.

"That must be Ralph with the turkey. They had a great sale on big birds at Jerry's." Paulette gave her a warm smile. Ralph was a quiet man, very much unlike his son, Jack. Although, looking at Ralph was like looking at a version of Jack through a Time Machine, thirty years from now.

"You'll come for Christmas dinner this year, won't you?" Paulette said, taking Holly's hands between hers. Holly's mouth dried up.

"Um maybe," she replied noncommittally.

Paulette puckered her lips. Holly looked down, not

wanting to see the disappointed look on Paulette's face. But Holly wasn't quite ready to face the holiday, or the holiday cheer without her mom quite yet.

She loved the season, but the day itself she usually spent alone. She would book a bus ticket into the city and spend the day people watching. There were usually fathers desperately shopping for a specific china glazed doll, the latest and greatest toy for that year, lovers holding hands in holiday bliss, children running with the smile of Christmas break on their faces.

She would get a coffee or hot chocolate at a cafe and sit for hours, then once the shops closed down, the city went quiet, and the roads empty. She would rent a hotel room at one of the tallest towers she could find and stay in bed for the whole night, watching crappy cops and robbers shows.

And her dad, well, her dad just wasn't around. When he and her mom had divorced when Holly was young, he had moved out to the big city and had never looked back. He had his new family and she wasn't a part of it.

Holly jumped, lost in thought, as Ralph came in the door with a very large wrapped frozen turkey and several bags of groceries piled in his arms.

"You wouldn't believe the price of these things." He said gruffly, plopping the large bird and bags on the granite island in front of Holly. He gave his wife a quick peck on the cheek.

"Oh hello, Hol." He said, nodding at her, not surprised to find her sitting there.

"And look who I found at the store," Ralph said as the door opened again and in came Jack with another bag of grocery bags. His eyes widened for a fraction of a second as he saw Holly in the kitchen.

Holly tensed. She hadn't seen or spoken to Jack since the diner, and they didn't exactly leave things well between them.

She should have known that she might run into him here. But her feet had carried her to her nearest source of comfort anyways.

Paulette and Ralph busied themselves with putting away the groceries as Jack set the final bags down on the island. Ralph grumbled about the cost of groceries these days as Paulette nodded along in agreement, responding back little *'oh isn't that just the truth's* and *'um hum's* every once in a while.

Jack came to sit beside Holly, taking in her face that was swollen from her cry earlier. His brow furrowed.

"What's happened?" He said, quietly enough for just Holly to hear. "Nothing." She responded, fiddling with a ring around her finger. His eyes darkened for a moment.

"Was it that guy–"

"I didn't mean to intrude–"

They both spoke at once. Jack was looking intently at her, his expression unreadable.

"Simon?" Holly spoke, "oh, no, he was fine actually."

Jack was quiet, before nodding as if confirming something in his mind.

"I wanted to talk to you about the other night actually." Holly felt her heart start to beat a little faster. She wasn't sure exactly what she wanted to talk about. What exactly to say. *Did you feel the thing I felt in the diner with the eyes and the heart thumping,* felt a little too indirect. *Hey, wanna date,* didn't quite feel right either.

"Don't worry about it. It was nothing," Jack said dismissively. *Nothing.* So it was *nothing* to him. Holly frowned, biting her lip. She felt the bottom of her heart fall out. Maybe she had imagined the moment between her. Maybe he had decided that the cute waitress was for him after all. Not that she could say much. She also had been seeing Simon.

"Hol, are you going to stay for dinner?"

"No," Holly responded a little too quickly. Her head shot up.

Paulette's eyes widened in question at Holly's abrupt behavior.

"No, I've got a few things to do… around the house. I should probably go now." She hoped that sounded convincing.

"Jack, dear, walk Holly home."

"Sure, Mom," Jack said, squeezing her shoulder as he walked past her.

"Oh no, that's not really necessary," Holly said, half heartedly waving her arms, but she knew that Paulette wouldn't take no for an answer. As kids, she also would also make Jack walk her home if she was ever over after school. Jack wouldn't hear it either, she knew.

Jack grabbed her coat and held it open for her to put her arms through. She mumbled thanks as she put on her coat.

❄

They walked down the street in silence. Holly chewed her lip. It wasn't an uncomfortable silence, but Holly couldn't help but think there were unsaid words between them. She could feel the tension in her shoulders build the further they walked without words. Each step without conversation making the last all the more painful.

"You're mad," Holly said finally.

"What?" Jack said. He stoped in his tracks.

"You've not texted me, or been by the shop."

"Was I supposed to have been by the shop? Also, you also haven't texted me?" Jack crossed his arms.

Holly opened and closed her mouth several times, trying to find the words to say anything.

"Like I said," Jack said. "It was nothing. I just didn't like that guy mistreating you." He shrugged and turned to continue down the street. Eyes forward. Holly snuck a look at Jack. He didn't look mad. She released a breath. He had slowed his pace, as he usually did when they walked together so that she wasn't practically running to catch up to him.

It had just snowed the night before, which left everything covered in glistening crystals of snow.

They walked through the streets of the town. The town was lit up with Christmas lights and large blow-up snow people. Most of the retail stores were closed at this time of day but the Cafes and restaurants that lined the streets were busy with friends and families celebrating the season. The schools had been let out this week, so the snow covered streets were busier than usual with kids running up and down them in coloured snow suits and puff topped hats.

"It's a beautiful evening–" Holly had settled on saying as they stopped at one of the pedestrian lights. She fiddled with the scarf around her neck.

Jack looked down at her, considering for a moment. His eyes swept over her.

"Yeah," He responded, putting his hands in his jacket pockets, and shrugging. Not a man of many words tonight apparently.

Holly gave him a small smile, thankful that the silence had ended.

"Jack?"

"Yeah."

"I just wanted to say–" as she felt her leg slip out from under her. Her foot slipped on ice that was hidden underneath the freshly fallen snow.

Jack caught her.

His strong hands warm and firm against her waist. Her heart quickened for a moment as their eyes met. He was dangerously close. Too close. He smelled slightly of cedarwood and the smoke of a campfire. He must have been woodworking earlier in the day. She remembered him telling her at some point that he had taken up the hobby.

Jack pulled her closer, steadying her on her feet.

His hands lingered on her waist, where she was keenly aware of how his fingers pressed into her. Her eyes flicked down to his lips. She sucked in a breath and she could swear that his eyes did the same. Holly only now realized how well built Jack was. His strong arms kept her steady.

"Jack?" She said, her voice uncertain. His gaze darkened on her and a little thrill of excitement went through her. And it occurred to Holly all at once that being held by Jack didn't feel weird.

Suddenly he spun her, and Holly gave a squeak as the world exploded with shards of white. A snowball collided with Jack's back as he sheltered her in his arms. He whipped his head in the direction of the attack. Three more balls of snow came pelting towards them.

Quickly, he released her, caught one in the air, and flung the ball back in the direction of three snot-nosed kids who all shrieked as the ball hit one of them square in the chest. Holly couldn't help but notice the cold absence of where his hands had held her.

"Attack," one of the kids yelled in a battle cry as the kids all ducked behind some forts built up from packed snow.

"Crap," muttered Jack as he pulled Holly behind a poorly constructed snowman that was built up against a brick wall.

"Death," cried another kid as several snowballs came hurling towards them. Jack pulled her close to him, using his body to shield her where the snowman could not. Flicks of cold licked Holly's cheeks as the snowballs collided with the snowman. Jack pulled her tight, bringing his jacket around her to shield her further. A hot flush came across Holly's cheeks, her hands pushed against his firm chest. Holly couldn't help but press her fingers against his shirt, her thumb finding the edge of his pectoral muscle. She bit her lip.

She knew he was strong, but Jack was ripped. She could feel his pectoral flex against her ministrations. He sucked in a breath and his fingers tightened against her.

"Braxton, Kayle, Beckaleigh. Knock it off. It's *not* the time," he yelled back at the kids as another slew of snowballs pelted down on them.

"Never surrender," yelled one of the kids.

"Wait, I think there may be a civilian casualty," yelled back another.

"She's with *him.*"

Holly couldn't help but have her jaw open. These kids *knew* Jack. This was a targeted attack.

"Death–"

"Death–"

"Death!"

Jack cursed under his breath.

"You know these kids?" Holly hissed.

"We're going to have to make a run for it," Jack said as another round of snowballs came pelting down.

"Do you see that picnic table over there, with the wooden snowman?" Holly nodded.

"When I say go, sprint for it." He said, looking at me seriously, while gathering a large snowball from the snowman in front of them.

"They're just kids," Holly said.

"Not just kids," Jack said, narrowing his eyes. "They're little unrelenting menaces."

He gathered another large snowball, making the snowman look lumpy and bumpy from where he had harvested the snow.

"You ready?" Jack said, spinning her around so she faced the picnic table. Jack peeked around the corner, waiting for the optimal moment where the kids were re-loading on snowballs.

"Go," Jack whispered in her ear, Holly could feel his breath hot on her, feeling the smile on his lips.

She sprinted as fast as she could towards the shelter. Balls of snow flew past her and she heard the kids shriek as one made impact.

Holly screeched to a stop as a snowball hit just in front of her. She squeaked as it exploded, showering her with specks of cold snow. The sign was still another fifteen feet from her. She didn't know if she could make it without being pelted. She looked quickly over at the kids.

There were two boys and one girl. One boy with ginger hair and a face full of freckles was currently focused on Jack, hurling over snow balls while tucked behind a large pile of snow. The other boy was smaller with long, almost black hair who was quickly forming balls and collecting them up in little pyramid shaped piles next to their snow fort. The last was a girl in a bright pink jacket and pigtails who was looking directly at Holly.

Holly looked down at the girl who had a freshly made snowball in her hand, ready to throw. *Crap.* Holly jumped backward as a snowball the girl was holding collided with the exact spot where she had been standing. She narrowed her eyes. *This wasn't going to work. She would never make it the extra feet to the shelter.*

The girl's eyes widened with surprise as Holly grabbed a fist full of snow. The snow prickled against her bare skin. Ice clumps in the snow were hard against her hand. She winced as she quickly formed the ball and threw it in the direction of the girl.

The girl gave a quiet shriek and then a giggle as the ball

collided with her snow fort. Holly quickly crouched down, taking the distraction to run towards the sign all while grabbing another first full of snow from the ground. The snow was fresher there and it hurt less to gather.

She formed the ball quickly. The sign was so close, just a few more steps. An almost occult feeling of imminent impact came over her as she dove towards the sign, blindly chucking the freshly made ball in the direction of the little girl's fort.

The two balls of show collided together, showering the area with bits of white. Holly had made it to the wooden snowman sign in time. She let out a sigh of relief.

"A formidable enemy." She heard the girl say and Holly couldn't help but smile. She warmed her hands together, wiping the water from the melted snow against the fabric of her coat. She blew breath on her hands to quicken the warming, rubbing them quickly against each other. How she wished she had put on gloves before she left the house this evening.

Holly braved peeking behind the wooden snowman as she heard a chorus of cries and shrieks. Jack had somehow gotten a hold of a large bucket, like the kind you would find at a home renovation store, and had filled it to the brim with snow. He had managed to make his way over to where the boys were and dunked the entire bucket of snow on the boys' heads.

"That is so not fair."

"You cheated."

Jack stood there triumphantly with his hands on his hips.

But just as Holly felt like the attack was over, she felt a smack of something hit her head, then she felt cold and then pain. She took a step back and her foot hit a slip of ice. The skating injury on her hip throbbed and the muscle gave way. She was falling. Her arms pinwheeled around as she tried to catch herself, her side hit the ground hard and she heard a crack of something bony as her shoulder hit the concrete curb of the sidewalk. A shot of pain was sent through her arm.

"Oh gosh, oh gosh, oh gosh." The girl came running over as Holly went down.

"Are you okay?" she asked, bringing two mittened hands up to her mouth. Holly sat there a moment in a daze, the pain from her arm becoming stronger as she tried to pull herself to a seat. She hissed in a breath.

"Jack." She heard the little girl yell.

"Jack, help, quick. I'm so sorry. I didn't think she would fall."

Holly clutched her arm, trying to roll out her shoulder. She sucked in another breath as pain shot through her arm once more.

"It's okay. I'm fine," she tried to say as Jack and the two boys came running over.

"Way to go Beckaleigh," the boy with freckles said as he shoved the girl, who shoved him back.

"It's not like I meant for her to fall, she looked more… more *stable* than that." the girl retorted back.

Thanks. Holly thought as she rubbed her arm. Not only did she fall once, but twice. She cursed the little black boots that she had decided to put on this morning. They looked so cute, but decidedly they were more of a fashion boot than an actual winter boot. The slick flat soles did nothing for traction in the snow and they had betrayed her twice in thirty minutes. Holly swore that she would be throwing out the boots as soon as she was home and would be looking online for a better, even cuter, pair. This time with an actual sole.

"Are you alright?" Jack asked softly as he inspected her, his eyes running over her for harm.

"I think so," she responded, trying to push herself up. She

let out a cry as pain shot through her arm once more. *Stupid arm*, she thought. Jack gave her a look with a raised brow.

"I don't think so," he said, then, leaning down he swept his hands underneath her legs and shifted her good arm around his shoulders. He picked her up off the ground as if she weighed nothing. Holly tried to protest but the look he gave her opened no doors for debate.

"Lift with your knees, not your back." One of the kids recited as the others nodded decidedly in agreement. She could practically hear Jack's eyes roll in his head.

"Can you kids run home and ask your mom to call the doctor's office and let them know that they'll have a late night patient come in?" The two boys nodded, both with a serious look on their faces.

"Rodger," said the boy with the ginger hair, giving Jack a salute before pulling the other little boy and girl to follow. The little girl pushed off the others, shaking her head.

"No, I'll stay with the patient. It's my duty after all." Jack opened his mouth to protest, but then decided it would be easier not to fight it. Jack turned with Holly securely in his arms, Beckaleigh in tow, and started to walk towards the medical office in town.

❄

The walk to the medical office was quiet.

Beckaleigh led the way, shoo-ing out the way of anyone walking who may have been walking on the same side of the sidewalk and therefore, according to her, *in the way.* Holly's cheeks were warm as she hid her face in Jack's jacket. The sun had set and the air had a frigidness to it that was starting to seep into her bones. The warmth from his chest was comforting.

Her arm throbbed.

The medical office was a small one story building, with a square wooden facade. It had the words 'COAL RIVER MEDICAL' hand painted in an old pinstripe style on the top of the building.

Jacked rapped on the door with the hand that supported Holly's back, twisting them so he could reach. Holly looked up at Jack, meeting his eyes before quickly looking away. He had carried her the whole way, not stopping or appearing to get tired in the least. It was like something out of a Jane Austin movie. Like he was Colonel Brandon and she was Marianne. He *was* a little younger than Colonel Brandon.

A light flicked on in the office and a man in a crisp white coat over a tweed shirt and blue trousers unlocked and opened the door. He had dark brown hair that was squashed to the side as if he had just been asleep. He wore a pair of turtle shell spectacles over his crisp green eyes.

Holly was surprised. Doctor Veronica Elliot had been the residing doctor in Coal River for many years. She had heard a rumor that she had been looking to retire soon, but she hadn't heard about this new doctor yet. Which was odd, considering the rate at which gossip spread in this town.

"You must be our patient." The man had a soft and inviting voice. He held the door open for Jack to step through and led the way to a small exam room. The doctor motioned for Jack to set Holly down on the exam table.

"I am Dr. Nicholas Beck, I see that you may have injured your arm. Can you tell me what happened?"

Beckaleigh interrupted before Holly was able to answer.

"Oh it's all my fault Doctor. But really, it was the midst of battle and we were on the brink of defeat. I hadn't thought about the ice, although my mom is always telling me about the ice." The doctor gave a thin lipped smile.

"Thank you for sharing that," the doctor said. "Why don't we give the patient a little bit of privacy," He motioned to the door. Jack ushered Beckaleigh back into the waiting room. The doctor closed the door behind them. Holly could hear Beckaleigh talking from inside the room, talking about battle strategies and the serious threat of ice. She could just imagine the look on Jack's face as his ear was talked off by the battle enthusiastic kid.

"Thank you," Holly said as the doctor turned back to her.

"I don't know if you caught anything from that, but yes, I slipped. On a patch of ice under the snow. I think my shoulder hit the curb." The doctor probed and manipulated her arm a few different ways.

"I also fell a few days ago, while skating, and I think I injured my hip. Nothing serious. And then the snowball hit me at a funny angle and down I went." She shrugged. The doctor looked at her with a raised eyebrow but simply asked her where she hurt herself then.

"I swear I don't usually fall this much," Holly said meekly, pointing to her right hip.

When the exam was complete he turned to her and said, "Well, I don't think it is broken. But it seems like you have a soft tissue injury. I would recommend to ice it and rest, at least for the next few days."

Holly nodded , shrugging on her jacket. The doctor got up to open the door.

"Thanks so much," she said. He gave her a soft smile back and she left the room.

Jack and Beckaleigh were waiting for her in the small room at the front of the building. Jack looked up at her expectantly as she entered, ignoring Beckaleigh who was now onto the subject of icicles and how they were an impalement risk.

"Not broken, but a little bruised," she said to Jack's expectant face and she could have sworn that he almost gave a little sigh of relief. Jack then looked down at Beckaleigh, who had gone silent. She was looking down at her hands. He nudged her softly.

"I'm sorry we drew you into the battle… and that you got hurt," she said, looking up at Holly. Small tears were forming in her eyes as she stuck out her bottom lip and Holly felt a swell of her own emotions.

"I accept your apology," Holly said, giving the girl a sincere smile. Beckaleigh ran over with her arms open wide for a hug. She collided with Holly, who let out a small noise of pain. Doctor Beck gave a small cough.

"Rest." He reminded Holly.

"Sorry," Beckaleigh said quietly, not releasing Holly but holding her a little less tight.

Jack went over to Doctor Beck and shook his hand.

"Thanks so much, Nick. How have you been settling in?" Doctor Beck pulled him in and gave Jack a pat on the back.

"Good. It's been busy with all of the paperwork to take over the practice, and the office is a lot smaller than my old one in the city. But now that I've seen my first patient, I'm sure I'll get into the swing of things soon."

Nick? Not Dr. Beck? Holly's eyebrows raised. Jack had never mentioned that he had a doctor friend. By the way they interacted, there was clear history of friendship.

"Do you know each other?" Holly blurted out before she could stop herself. She clapped her mouth shut as both men looked over at her and then at each other.

Jack gave her a smile.

"Hol, you don't know everything about me." Holly stuck her tongue out at him, and he ruffled her hair.

"Hol? As in Holly?" Doctor Beck, *Nick*, said, looking between Holly and Jack with a look of understanding cross his face.

"Yup, that's me," Holly said, furrowing her brow. Jack had

clearly mentioned her, though she couldn't have said the same about Nick.

"We met back in college," Nick said. *Ah, the dark days.* When Holly and Jack graduated high school the both of them went their separate ways when they went off to college. Jack had gone off to the West Coast, to a fancy college, Stanford, and Holly had stuck to a local community college. Back then Holly had thought that had been the end of their friendship. Jack didn't have social media, so bar the major holidays like Christmas, when Jack would make his annual visit to his hometown and their families would get together, Jack and Holly didn't talk.

Holly was in a relationship with, *he-who-must-not-be-named*, as well. So even during those visits, Holly was so wrapped up in her relationship, and its failings, to connect back with Jack. Those were what Holly now called the dark days in their relationship.

It wasn't until Jack had moved back after both of them had graduated college that they had reconnected. But neither of them had talked about those years. There wasn't really a point. What would they talk about other than beer pong parties and the philosophy classes that neither of them remembered.

Holly reached out her hand.

"Nice to formally meet you. Holly. Holly MacIntosh," she said with a large grin on her face. Nick looked surprised for a moment, looking between Holly's outstretched hand and Jack, as if wondering how in the world Holly's ball of sunshine energy could possibly be friends, let alone close friends, with Jack. Jack shrugged as if to say he didn't know either. A large smile broke out on Nick's face in return as he took her hand in his, giving her a strong shake in return.

"It's nice to formally meet you as well." He laughed.

Holly shook his hand enthusiastically. Beckaleigh, who had detached herself from Holly's midriff, gave a big yawn.

"I think we had better get these girls home," Jack said, noting the increasingly tired look on Beckaleigh's face. Jack scooped up Beckaleigh into his arms, who almost immediately laid her head on his shoulder. Nick nodded, walking the group to the door of the clinic.

"Say hi to your family for me," Nick said, as he waved goodbye and closed the doors to the clinic behind them. They began walking down the street towards where Holly presumed it was Beckaleigh's house.

"Daddy." Beckaleigh sighed, snuggling into Jack's arms. And Holly's stomach went cold.

✳

Daddy?

Holly's eyebrows rose to her hairline.

What in the world? There's no way in the world that those kids could be Jack's kids. Jack did just say that she didn't know everything about him. What else was Jack hiding from his days in university? *Secret triplets?*

There was no way. But looking at the two of them now though, it looked as if Beckaleigh had done this before, she was very comfortable in his arms. There was also an air of resemblance in the way they looked too. Who was the mother? She understood never telling her about a handsome doctor friend, but his secret kids and the mother of his children never being mentioned. Oh god, he did go away sometimes. Was that him visiting them?

She narrowed her eyes at Jack. He looked back at her.

"How exactly do you know those kids?" she asked, hoping her voice still sounded casual. Jacked looked back at Holly, his forehead wrinkled.

"That's a little hard to explain," Jack said and Holly fought hard for her mouth to not hang open.

Oh gosh. They were *his* kids. She could feel herself panicking. Jack was right. If she didn't know about his kids, his literal offspring, she didn't know him at all. She felt a sting of betrayal. There was no way that she could have kept a secret like this from him. How could he have done the same? No wonder the kids were so desperate for his attention to attack him in the street. They were desperate to know their father.

They turned onto Holly's street. The street was in the older part of town, where the houses were mostly small and historic, with a hedge or small picket fence surrounding the perimeter. Every house on the street was decorated fully with lights, lanterns and the occasional snowman. It was a part of the town where it was almost seen as a community requirement to decorate during the holiday season and was highly frowned upon not to.

"Try to," Holly said, fiddling with button of her coat. Holly felt her words betray her. It was none of her business as Jack had never told her. But she couldn't help it. She had to know, in some self-deprecating way, what happened for him to keep this secret from her for *years*. His family must have been in on the deception too, which would make sense. A secret family, out of web-lock nonetheless. It would be the talk of the town for weeks. Months even. Years.

"Well–"

Jack paused for a moment, looking unsure of how to begin or if to begin. His brows furrowed. He took a deep breath. This was it. He would tell her the devastating secret of a hidden family.

"Do you remember a few years ago when my grandfather remarried? Beverly."

Oh.

Holly nodded slowly. Jack hoisted Beckaleigh slightly so she was higher in his arms. The little girl didn't stir at all.

"Well, Beverly was a little younger than my grandfather. And she and my grandfather had kids. So these kids... are... technically..."

"Your aunt and uncles," Holly finished his sentence.

Jack looked stained.

"Yeah," He said after a moment. Holly looked at the little girl who gave out a big sigh. Holly lowered her voice a little.

"So Beverly must be–"

"Two years older than me. Yeah," Jack said, and they both let out a little laugh at the absurdity. They continued on their walk as they continued onto Holly's street.

"That must have been hard on your family," Holly said as they reached the curb of her house. They both stood there. Silent. Where they had stood many times before.

"Mostly on my mom, yeah. Having your father marry somebody as young as your child is probably weird. But Bev is actually a really nice lady. And they're generally good kids. If not a bit... enthusiastic" He pulled his lips in. Holly could see there was love there– a love for the three rambunctious children that had been placed in his life.

A warmth settled in the pit of her stomach as she looked at Jack holding the child and she knew then that he would make an excellent father one day.

Holly opened the gate of the her fence and said goodnight to Jack.

EIGHTEEN DAYS UNTIL
CHRISTMAS

✻

*B*irds chirped happily outside of Holly's window. Holly let out a groan as her body ached, cursing the birds for their cheer on what was not a cheery morning. The only solace Holly had was the mountain of fluffy and warm blankets piled around her. Her whole body ached and she wouldn't be surprised if she was covered in faint purple bruises.

One arm reached out, fumbling to find the bottle of pain reliever pills she had stashed on her side table. Holly cursed as she knocked it over with a clang. She poked a head out from the covers, her hair a rat's nest of tangles. Locating the bottle she poured one out into her hand and swallowed it with a sip of stale water.

She sat back in bed, relishing in the warmth for a few more minutes. She could stay in bed forever, right? Maybe she should text Mia to open the store without her. She felt like she had been run over by a train, and then the train switched directions and ran over her again.

She grabbed her phone from the side table and flicked off the charger.

One text message from Mia, one from Jack, and one from Simon.

Holly opened the text from Simon.

```
(S) Hey beautiful. Looking
forward to our date tomorrow ;)
```

Date? Oh right. The date she had agreed to go on. He wanted to take her to dinner and talk about the fair. Holly pinched the bridge of her nose.

Her phone buzzed and Holly's eyebrows rose. Oliver Kilton.

```
(O) Are you still interested in
meeting today?
```

Holly rubbed her temple. She had completely forgotten that she had set up a meeting with him. She looked over at her wardrobe. The black folder with all of the information about her shop was there. She would bring it with her. At least she had done all of the work to show off her business. She wasn't going to sell, but perhaps she could convince this company to invest into her business and she could get some money for the repairs.

She opened the text from Jack.

```
(J) How's the arm?
```

Holly smiled. Short, simple and to the point. That was Jack. She rolled her shoulder a little bit. The pain relievers seemed to be kicking in, thankfully.

```
(H) I was contemplating
amputation, but it seems a bit
better after some drugs.
```

```
(J) Riffraff, MacIntosh. So old
lady Greywell was right, this
town is going to the pits.
```

Holly fought back a grin.

> (H) It's a Christmas miracle
> I've not been chased out of
> town.

> (J) It's only a matter of days
> now. I've even heard rumors of
> rogue snowball fights breaking
> out in the streets.

> ...

> (J) Sorry about that btw. The
> triplets got a very stern
> talking to when I dropped
> Beckleigh at their hotel, so
> rest assured it won't be
> happening again. She's really
> taken a liking to you. I heard
> her lecturing her brothers about
> keeping the princess safe when I
> was leaving.

> ...

> (J) Hey, so I won't be able to
> drop by the shop today, but
> would you like to drop by my
> cabin tomorrow after you close?
> I've got something I'd like to
> show you if you're available.

The cabin? In the five years that he had been back in town, she had never been to Jack's cabin. It was a outside of town, in the woodsy area, so it was usually easier to go to her place.

It was apparently a real dump when he had bought it for pennies and he had been renovating it for ages. It was also in the middle of nowhere. So although she had heard endlessly about how much of a steal it was, she wasn't convinced that the location made it worth it. It somehow suited Jack's mythos.

The beautiful lumberjack who lived in the woods. She could almost hear the laugh of the waitress who was fawning all over him the other day. She would probably think that it was super hot of him. Holly rolled her eyes.

She had always imagined it was decorated in flannel and deer antlers. Not that Jack hunted. Or at least she *thought* he didn't hunt. Fished, maybe? Oh God. Was Jack the type to have a picture of a fish on his online dating profile? Probably. Holly let out a huff of a laugh. That and he probably a picture of his pick-up truck and some kind of pick up line like a quote from *Walden Pond* about the 'tonic of wildness.'

Tomorrow night. Holly furrowed and then unfurrowed her brow, remembering words from Mia that worry faces caused wrinkles between the brows. She was supposed to go to dinner with Simon. But she could probably ask for a late dinner and head to Jack's cabin right after she closed the shop.

She felt a strange feeling of honor being invited out to Jack's cabin that she couldn't pass up. Not after she had to endure hearing about his renovations for the past few years.

Holly opened the text from Mia.

> (M) Hey Holly,
> I'm feeling a little under the weather today.
> Think you can open the shop without me today?

Ugh. Mia had been sniffling yesterday, so Holly wasn't surprised that she was sick.

Holly pulled off the covers and tried not to hiss at the cold air that accosted her. So much for taking a break today. So was the life of an owner-operator of a store. There were no days off, there were no late days. There were only long days.

❄

Ro was next to Holly as they walked down the street. She had convinced Holly that they should do some window shopping after work to cheer her up.

"So tell me about this date with Simon. He seemed cute enough when we went out to the pub. And he wouldn't stop asking about you when you failed to show up." Ro waggled her eyebrows at her.

"He's nice," Holly responded, shrugging.

"Nice," Ro looked up through her lashes at Holly. "Never have I heard a more passionate retelling of a date."

"I don't know much about him yet. But I am getting to know him. He's not a no yet." Holly said, trying to satisfy Rowena's curiosity. She had not told Ro about her thoughts about Jack. She probably wouldn't ever either. Ro and Jack were like oil and water.

"You could always sell pictures of your feet," Ro said, her flowing skirts dragged in the snow behind them. She let out a noise of exasperation as she shook them out and bundled them in her arms. They had stopped in front of one of the town boutiques. Unfortunately, with the Town of Cole River being a tourist destination, most of the boutiques were way out of Holly and Ro's budget. But they still had fun shopping the windows, maybe even trying somethings on if they were feeling wild.

"Right," Holly deadpanned.

"No. In all seriousness. I've heard that people can make a killing online. And you've got cute feet." Ro hooked her arm in Holly's.

"I'm not selling photos of my feet." Holly twisted her finger around her plaited hair. It wasn't that Holly hadn't thought about different side hustles to help out with expenses, but that particular side hustle was too much for

Holly. It seemed like a lot of work. Getting manicures all of the time, having an online presence. No. Holly would not be starting a foot pic side hustle.

"Mia started a social media account for the shop," she said changing the topic and tapping on the glass of the shop window. Ro gave a feigned hum of interest. Holly wasn't even convinced that social media was the cure to her financial woes. But Mia was willing to set it up and post, and she appreciated the gusto she was putting into finding a solution. She pointed at a Christmas apron with little nutcrackers that hung in the shop window.

"Cute," Ro remarked about the apron. She walked over to the door of the shop and ushered Holly inside.

She had kept the text conversation she was having with the investor to herself. She hadn't told a single soul yet. She felt like if she said it outloud that a mob might show up to her house with pitchforks.

"Actually, I was going to go into the city this—" Holly ran face first into something firm. Holly hissed as the bruise on her shoulder throbbed by the impact. Her hands came up investigating what she had run into. A chest? A chest that felt oddly familiar. Holly looked up to see Jack standing there with a smirk on this face.

Holly jumped back.

"I'm beginning to think I need to buy you a helmet." Jack crossed his arms.

"Hello lumberjack," Ro drawled out, stepping out from behind Holly and into the shop. Ro was definitely goading Jack. She knew just how much Jack hated being called lumberjack.

"Hello town witch," he responded back. They had this rivalry going since they were in high school. As if they needed to one up each other constantly, but they endured each other's presence for Holly's sake.

"I thought you were supposed to be resting," Jack said, turning towards Holly, eyeing her to make sure she was still completely intact and not about to fall over.

"Yes. I am. Kind of. Mia is sick so I still had to go into work. And then Ro wanted to go shopping. I've got this business meeting later as well." Holly brought a hand to the back of her neck and cringed internally. It didn't sound great now she said it out loud. She never had been good at sitting still. There was just too much at stake.

"Weren't you supposed to be doing something today?" Holly asked, changing the subject.

"I got roped into taking the kids out shopping for Christmas presents for their parents," Jack said, nodding to inside the store.

"How very domestic," Ro mumbled and Holly shot her a look.

'Be nice.' She mouthed at Ro.

"Nick asked about you, he was wondering how you were feeling," Jack asked. Ro looked at Holly suspiciously. Holly hadn't quite gotten the chance to tell Ro about the doctor's visit last night. There hadn't seemed like a good time. And Ro was always on about Holly working all of the time and not taking time for herself. As both Jack and Ro looked at her, Holly suddenly felt hot. Like a spotlight was shining down from the heavens onto her.

A crash of breaking glass rang through the shop. Their heads whipped up towards where the Beckaleigh, Kayle and Braxton stood around a stone plinth with the pieces of an expensive looking vase lay at the base. The triplets paled as they saw Jack approaching. Beckaleigh looked accusingly at her brothers, who held up their hands as if being arrested.

"The vase just went crash–"

"It was such a pretty vase–"

"Braxton was getting away–"

"I really didn't touch it–"

The triplets spoke over each other and a slew of excuses and blame flew out of their mouths.

Jack kneeled down, picking up the pieces of the vase. He looked up as tears had started to form in Braxton eyes. The boy huffed as the droplets rolled down his cheek.

Jack wiped his face, giving him a kiss on the top of his head.

"I love you more than the broken vase," he said gently, reassuring the kids who had started to puff up in the way that kids did when they were overwhelmed.

The statement hit Holly like a truck. Growing up, Holly would have been berated by her father. He believed that kids should feel the consequences of their actions. He would have practically pulled her by her ear out the shop and she would have received the cold shoulder from him for the rest of the week.

The kids all rushed Jack in a hug around his waist.

"Now. Tell me what happened."

They all started talking at once again, and Jack held up a single finger to silence them.

"One at a time."

Kayle started. He explained that he had found a necklace that was a perfect gift for their Mom, but Braxton had taken it before Kayle had a chance to bring it to Jack and so Kayle took chase. Braxton had been looking at Kayle when he ran into Beckaleigh, who had stepped backwards and bit the plinth. Jack just stood there, listening. And he actually looked like he was listening to what they were saying.

"And what do you think should have happened differently so that the vase didn't break?"

Holly's watch buzzed and a meeting reminder flashed on the screen. Holly looked apologetically at Ro. She put a hand on Jack's arm.

"I've got to run."

Both Jack and Ro gave her the same look as she dashed out of the shop.

❄

Holly couldn't shake the feeling from the store. Jack had been so patient with the children even when they had broken, an arguably very expensive item in the store. She remembered looking at the vase price at one of the previous window shopping adventures that she and Ro had gone on, and she was pretty sure there were at least three zeros in the price.

Holly looked down at her phone as she leaned over her steering wheel and backed her car into a parking spot on the side of the road. The city was always a busy place, especially downtown. She hated driving into it and avoided it at almost all cost. Except this one. She had a meeting with Oliver, and she couldn't risk anybody from the town seeing her meet him. He had offered to meet her in town, but she insisted on meeting in the city instead.

Holly tapped her phone. She scrolled through her messages and landed on her last message with her dad. God. Had it been six months since she had texted him last? Her last phone call had been weird. Her thumb hovered over the conversation for a second, before tapping it. The message opened. She fought back a scoff as she saw he left her on read for those six months. It was a thank you after he had wished her a happy birthday. She asked how his week was going. But no reply. She felt the sting of rejection flare up in her.

Holly almost tapped out the message. But then she remembered Jack's interaction with the triplets and she knew deep down that she wanted a relationship with her father. She wasn't a child any longer and she was old enough that maybe she could be the one to kindle that relationship and make it better. Maybe if she just tried a little harder to forgive him, he would want her.

She tapped a few words and hit send.

> (H) Hey Dad, I am in the city
> today and I was wondering if you
> would like to have dinner. I
> know it's last minute, but I
> should be free after six. Please
> let me know, I would love to
> see you.

There. The olive branch was olive branching. She tucked her phone into her pocket before leaving the car.

❄

The building was shiny and tall. With light strips everywhere that made metal look amazing and your skin look like you'd just risen from the dead. Holly suddenly felt very underdressed as she walked past men and women in crisp designer suits. Her frilly jeans with embroidered daisies made her feel like a small-town girl in a very not small-town world.

She reached the concierge desk and gave a little cough to get the attention of the concierge working there. The staff was a well kept woman with a sharp nose and a thin face.

"I'm here to meet with Mr. Kilton, Oliver Kilton that is." The woman looked down her nose at Holly, giving her the distinct feeling that she was being evaluated. The woman turned as she audibly pressed a few buttons on the landline phone and talked to somebody on the other end.

"You can wait over there," the woman said, pointing to a cluster of very sculptural, yet uncomfortable looking couches.

"Thanks," Holly said, giving the woman a small smile before turning and finding a seat.

It wasn't long before she heard her name called. Her head shot up as she saw Oliver walk over to her. He pulled down the sleeves of his suit before extending a hand to her. She took it with a very firm shake. *How formal.* The man was tall and lean. The type of tall that would have you go, *'woah, you're tall'* the first time you met them.

"I made a reservation for us at *El Perro Pájaro*. It's this amazing little Mexican restaurant just down the street." Oliver put a hand out for Holly to go first towards the door.

"A reservation? Wait— sorry. No." Holly halted in her steps. "I can't stay for dinner. I have... other plans. This was just supposed to be a business meeting." She said the word slowly, looking him directly in the eye. *Good god. Was he trying to date her too?* She goes months without being on a single date and then all of a sudden she accidentally goes on *two* dates in one week. Dates that she didn't know were dates with dudes that she didn't have any interest in dating in the first place.

Oliver chuckled, pulling out his phone and sending a quick text message.

"No problem. I've changed our table to bar seating. We'll go for drinks." He looked at her like he could read her panicked thoughts.

"It's where we take all of our clients," he explained slowly. Holly felt her cheeks go red. Ok. She may have jumped to conclusions.

"Just drinks," she repeated.

"Just drinks."

❄

Oliver was more... human than she had anticipated. He didn't come across as the sleazy investor type that she had been preparing for. In fact, he didn't pressure her at all about selling. He just gave her the rundown of their firm. Listened to what she had to say about her business. In return, he had a few pamphlets for her to take home with her, along with a very branded pen. She would have to hide them in the house once she got home.

"You should really meet my boss." He said, waving the waiter down to get the bill. He took the last sip of his gin martini.

"She was actually born and raised in Cole River." Holly's eyes widened. He seemed pleased at her surprise. "Yeah, that's why she's so passionate about keeping the town afloat." He passed her a business card. It was a shiny metal, so you knew it was somebody important.

Marla Fairfax, CEO. Holly said a quiet thank you before putting the materials he had given her into her purse. *Fairfax?* She wasn't familiar with the name. Cole River was bigger than Holly sometimes gave it credit for. It was small, but not so small that she knew every family in town. Holly winced as she took another sip of the drink she had ordered. It was very spicy and very alcohol forward. Not the drink for her, but she was polite enough to try to finish it.

Holly pressed the button on the side of her watch.

No new messages.

The hour was getting late. The sky was turning a burnt orange. She hated driving in the dark. She guessed there would be no dinner with Dad. Holly suppressed a sigh and tried her hardest not to be hurt. She could feel a tension deep in her chest that was there frequently when she interacted with her father.

She slipped her phone out of her pocket and texted Ro.

> (H) Rom com movie marathon
> tonight?

It took Ro less than a minute to respond.

> (R) You're on. Already making
> the popcorn. Pick up some sweet
> treats on your way home?

Holly gave a small smile. She could always count on Ro to be there for her in her lowest moments, and boy did this one feel low.

As Oliver returned to the table his eyes swept over her expression, and a look of confusion settled onto his face.

"Is everything alright?" he asked. Holly got the impression that he was being genuine in his concern.

"Yeah," she said, schooling her face back into the cheery demeanor she had been showing off previously. "Just some canceled plans. I should probably be heading back into town before it gets too late. Thank you for meeting with me. You gave me a lot to think about."

Oliver nodded slowly.

"I'll walk you back to your car."

❄

*H*olly pressed a button labeled *All Wheel Drive* on her car as she turned onto a road that was not a road. It was more of a slew of gravel and snow. How in the world did Jack make this drive every day. She hoped that the button would save her. Did the button even do anything or was it just to make schmucks like herself feel better when going down a road like this where they had no business going down?

She felt the rear of her car start to slide sideways as she made a slight right turn to follow the road. She cursed the salesman who had convinced her that ALL SEASON tires were for all seasons and would be fine in winter. *Fine schmine*. The tires were not fine. They were slippery and slidey. This was exactly why she avoided diving in the winter. In town, the nearest grocery store was just a fifteen minute walk away.

But no. Jack had to live out in the woods. *Weirdo*.

Holly had spent the whole cursed day thinking about this moment— seeing Jack's cabin for the first time. She was a little less sore than earlier in the day, but she had a wicked purple bruise that was growing on the tip of her shoulder. It matched perfectly the one that graced her hip.

Holly gripped the steering wheel, her knuckles turned white from the pressure. She was not convinced that she would actually make it to his cabin without her car ending up in the ditch. She looked at her phone that was displaying the map to the cabin. Just another seven minutes. She took a deep breath in, trying to calm her nerves.

The forest got thicker around her as she drove closer to the cabin. A blanket of crystal white snow covered the tips of the pine and spruce forest. The underbrush was so thick that you couldn't even see the trunks of the trees. A deep fog seemed to be settling in. It would have been spooky if it wasn't so beautiful.

Quiet. It was so quiet.

She drove around another corner and said a prayer as she felt the wheel slip again. She turned another curve.

Then suddenly, there was a break in the trees, and out appeared the most perfect little lake. It was completely frozen over and was the clearest turquoise color in the center with banks of pure white. Bushes and trees lined the edge of the lake. The snow fog rolled over the frozen water in blusts of sparkling clouds. Holly sucked in a breath. It was devastatingly beautiful and private.

Holly could see a cabin with a private beach and wooden dock on the other side of the lake. That was Jack's cabin. He had never mentioned his own private lake before. She had a hunch she knew why. This was a slice of private paradise.

Though the lake was haunting in winter, it would be absolutely amazing in the hot summer. She could already imagine spending her days bathing by the banks of the lake in a bikini with a nice gin and tonic in her hand.

She gripped the steering wheel once more with a

renewed determination. She was almost there. The fog was getting thicker as she turned the final curve.

There it was, a two-story cabin with Jack's pickup truck parked in the front under a small shelter. The shelter had a corrugated roof to keep snow off of the vehicle.

She slammed her foot onto the break as she came up to the cabin and felt the brake lock. *Shit. Shit. Shit.* The vehicle wasn't slowing. Holly closed her eyes and pressed as hard as she could on her brakes. She waited for the inevitable thud that would come from hitting the back of Jack's car. She squeezed her eyes shut as much as she could, tensing. But the thud never came.

"Jesus, MacIntosh. Did you even pass driver's ed?" She heard Jack yell.

Holly opened one eye. The car had stopped. A few inches from the bumper of his truck. But the car had stopped. Jack was standing on the second-story balcony, looking wholly unimpressed. Holly rolled down the window, ignoring the plop of snow that landed inside her car as a result.

"You live in the middle of nowhere. On a road that has no business calling itself a road. I just about died on my way here, I hope you know." Holly yelled up.

Ugh, she hated winter driving. She took back everything she had thought about this beautiful property a moment before. It was a stupid property on a dangerous road. And Jack was insane for living here. He was insane for inviting her here. Jack disappeared inside the cabin and Holly pulled on her coat to get out of her car.

Holly walked to the front door. Her heart rate, which had settled from the almost accident moments before, started to beat loudly again. The property was bare of any holiday decor, apart from a single juniper wreath which was hung on the front door. Holly smiled a little. It was the wreath that Holly had given to Jack a week earlier. He had put it up, and on his front door no less. Holly was touched. She was half convinced that he would use it as fire starter.

Jack opened the front door, his broad frame filling out most of it. He was wearing a knit gray sweater and a pair of light-wash jeans. Holly was somewhat surprised that no flannel was in sight.

"I'm here. I made it. Miraculously." She shrugged as he moved aside to let her in.

Holly turned to let Jack pull her jacket off as tried her hardest not to let her jaw hang open.

The inside of the cabin was nothing like she had pictured. It looked so much bigger on the inside. The walls were vertical planks of wood that soared to a second story with a vaulted exposed beam ceiling. Inside there was an open stainless steel kitchen, just big enough that Holly could imagine having coffee and fritadas in the morning, and there was a small staircase to the right of it that led to a lofted area where Holly assumed Jack was when she arrived.

A large fireplace stood in the corner of the room with round gray stones extending up to the ceiling. Holly let a breath out. The side of the cabin that faced the lake held expansive windows that filled the wall and provided an unobstructed view. Snow had started to fall creating an even more beautiful landscape. The cabin was a perfect combination of modern, traditional and rustic.

The wooden walls filled the room with the most delicious smell of cedar wood. Holly bit back a smile as she spied a strangely modern rendition of a deer made of twisted cast iron hung on the wall. So she wasn't entirely wrong on the decor front, but she had to admit she had underestimated Jack.

"Damn, Jack. Where have you been hiding this place all along?" Holly said, giving him a playful bump with her hip.

She could see a look that resembled pride cross his face for a moment.

"Yeah? I only put the finishing touches on it this fall. I still need to put a railing on the stairs and there's a few more things that need final trim pieces. Half the rooms aren't even furnished." He brought one hand to rake through his blonde hair.

"Are you kidding me? No. It's perfect. You are going to be in so much trouble with Mrs. Greywell. But it is beautiful." Holly gave him a big smile. Jack was too modest sometimes. This place was incredible. Like magazine worthy incredible.

"Weren't you just telling me how it is a death trap to get here?" Jack teased, grinning back.

"Well. That fact remains true. It is a death trap road, but I suppose the best places are hard to get to. Mount Everest. Could die there. Mount Kilimanjaro. Lions. Gorillas. Potential death. Your cottage. That road. Death." She shrugged back as if it was just the truth.

Jack rolled his eyes at her.

"Sure, kid." He ruffled her hair like when they were teens. She let out an exaggerated gasp, fighting back the urge to push him away, reverting back to when they were kids. Jack let out a chuckle and she couldn't help but join in. Their laughs died out after a moment of self-indulgence. The sides of her mouth ached from smiling so much.

"Are you going to show me around this place? I've heard enough about it." She stuck her tongue out at him.

He nodded and she swatted at his hand as he tried to ruffle her hair once more. He gave her a small tour of the place and it was just as stunning as she thought initially. She had to admit. Jack had good taste. He skirted around the bedrooms, waving to them and casually mentioning there were three.

Three. That stuck out to Holly. Her gaze softened as he

was explaining how he designed the kitchen around some kind of organizational model-thingy. It was so clear to her now. He had designed this home for a family. For his family.

What type of woman would agree to live down here, she had no idea. It would have to be somebody as happy with a quiet and secluded life as he was. But it was sweet. Holly felt a pang of sadness that took her by surprise. She struggled to keep the smile on her face as he prattled on about stone countertops, but felt the corners of her mouth pull downward.

He had thought out every last detail of his life here. But she didn't know if it was the same as how she imagined her life. To give up the town? To live in the woods? She didn't know if she could do that. Jack stopped talking as he noticed the look on her face. And he raised an eyebrow.

"Hol? Are you ok? I'm probably talking about the kitchen too much, huh." Holly could see the nervousness in his face. He felt passionate about this place.

Holly shook her head. What was she thinking anyways. She wasn't his wife. Heck, they weren't even dating. Not even close to it. Maybe the pretty waitress at the dinner dreamed of a cabin in the woods like this. She didn't even know why it made her sad. Holly tensed her shoulders.

"It just seems like a waste all the way out here." She snapped her head down. Knowing that she was being wretched. Mean. Lashing out at because of the unpleasant feeling she was experiencing. She didn't dare look up at him and face the disappointment that might be on his face.

"Yeah, well, I like the quiet," he said, bringing his hands up in defense. She felt a buzz in her pocket and checked her watch.

SIMON

The name flashed on the face of the watch. She ignored

the incoming text message. She had told Simon that she was going to be late tonight and that a late dinner would work. However, it took her longer than she had anticipated to get here, with the snow and ice she was driving slowly.

"So what did you want to show me all the way out here anyways?" Holly said, spinning the ring on her finger.

"It's back here," he said, moving towards a door near the back leading out towards the lake. He grabbed her jacket and handed it to her before he pulled on his own.

Holly squinted from the reflection of the snow as they left the building. Jack had carved out a small path in the snow that led into the woods.

"This seems like the lead up to a murder mystery. Is this how I find out you're secretly an ax murderer?" Holly said.

"I'm ignoring that," Jack said as he placed a steadying hand on the small of her back and led her down the path. Holly raised an eyebrow.

"You don't have the best record for not slipping on icy paths," he said.

Holly bristled, but let him lead her down the path. The path diverted a few places to outbuildings. Holly paused at each fork in the path and Jack would gently guide her in the correct direction until they happened upon a long curved building with glass walls. Holly stopped in her tracks.

"Is that what I think it is?" Holly asked and Jack said nothing but grinned in response.

He pulled out a hoop of keys that jingled as he tried to find the correct one before sticking it in the lock and opening the door.

"I've been working on this for a while. I know that you've had a hard time finding suppliers in winter, especially being a local only shop."

"Local forward," Holly corrected.

"Local forward," Jack repeated.

Holly was hit by a blast of hot and humid air as she entered into a small chamber about six feet by six feet, on the other end was a set of thick plastic curtains.

"How is this even possible in winter?" Holly asked as Jack closed the door behind them. The greenhouse felt tropical, like she had just stepped out of an airplane in the Caribbean. There was no trace of the icy conditions outside.

Jack grabbed her coat and hung it on a row of hooks. They certainly didn't need them considering she was already sweating from the seonds that had passed in the building.

"The land has a natural spring, so this is all heated by steam and geo-thermal energy." Jack pulled back the plastic curtain and Holly was met with rows upon rows of flowers.

Holly brought a hand to her mouth. Her chest swelled. Each row contained a different flower species. There were anemone, ranunculus and lillies. She had no idea what to expect when Jack had invited her over, but this was certainly not it.

The air smelled of a sweet perfume. She walked over to a row of snapdragons and slid her hand along the cool metal of the troughs that held the plants. He had not once in all the times he had talked about his property mentioned a greenhouse, let alone a greenhouse filled with flowers.

"You're becoming a flower farmer?" Holly said, not sure how to react.

Jack shrugged.

"I am working on something special. Cover your eyes."

"More special than this?" she asked, twirling her finger around the room.

Jack nodded.

She covered her eyes obligingly with one hand as he led her down the rows. She felt a branches sweep past her as he guided her through the greenhouse. They stoped and he turned her, with his hands covering her shoulders.

"Open," he said in her ear. She could feel his breath hot against her neck and goosebumps covered her body. Holly was met with a single bush that had several crisp white roses. The buds were cupped together tightly with the petals having the slightest furl outward. They were so pure white they almost looked blue. The petals were lined with dew drops from the humidity making them shimmer like cut crystal.

"What did you do?" Holly said in absolute shock.

"I've been playing around with hybridization, crossing some of the species I have in the greenhouse." He grabbed a knife and cut a stem and presented it to Holly.

"I was thinking of calling them a snowdrop rose." He gave her a small smile as she took the stem from him. She twirled the stem in her fingers, opening the petals slightly.

"They're beautiful," she said softly, bringing the rose up to her nose.

"I didn't know that you knew how to do this. Or had an interest in it." She breathed in deeply, smelling its sweet scent. "What else are you hiding?" She crinkled her eyes at him.

"I am a florist's son as much as you are a florist's daughter." Jack looked over at the rows of flowers.

"Mom would drag us out to flower farms all over the east coast every summer. I guess some of it stuck," he said.

"I remember." Holly nodded. Paulette had been the procurer of plants when their parents had owned the shop. When Holly had taken it over she had decided to shift the focus to more local producers, especially as many of the original flower farmers were retiring and had children who didn't want to take over the farms. The original farmers had to shut down their businesses. Holly felt that it was more ethical to find local suppliers, but Holly didn't have time or a partner who could spend weeks and weeks to scour the country for other suppliers. So during the winter months, she had to resort to importing flowers.

Holly felt a sting at the edge of her eyes. She shoved the flower in her nose once more, turning away from Jack and towards the lanes of flowers. She hoped that Jack wouldn't notice the wetness forming in her eyes. Nobody had ever done something so significant for her before. Holly put the flower down before launching her arms around Jack.

Jack went still for a moment, before he wrapped his arms around her, holding her tight.

She buried her head into his chest, breathing in his scent.

"I made you a promise, didn't I?" Jack whispered into her hair.

Holly's eyes widened. *Promise?* Holly couldn't believe that he still held himself to it. It was back when they were kids, like little kids, and Holly's mom and dad had just gotten divorced.

Holly had been crying to herself in the back room of the shop when Jack had stumbled upon her. He wanted to back out at first, but he didn't chicken out in the face of a crying girl. Little Jack puffed out his chest and sat next to her. He had put a tentative hand on her back and she flung herself into his arms. Crying. He held her, like he held her now, tentatively rubbing her back until she had stopped crying.

"It's all my fault." Holly had said, as he let her wipe the tears from her eyes. She had cried to him about how her father had abandoned them for a new family and had left her and her mom behind. He had stuck out a pinky to her and she had crossed it with her own. He had promised her then that he would always be there to look after her.

As a child Jack was so tender and gentle.

It had never been brought up again, but Holly never forgot his kindness then. He had always been a guardian angel of sorts for her. Just always there when she really needed him.

"Thank you," she said into his chest. Her words muffled by his shirt. She looked up at him. His gaze softened for a split second. Her breath hitched in her throat as he held her.

His eyes locked on Hollys. They stood there in each other's arms.

Unconsciously, Holly tipped her chin up and she could have sworn his gaze flicked down to watch her tongue wet her lips.

Jack brushed his thumb over her lower back, sending a thrill through her body. She leaned into his touch. He brought a hand up to her chin, cradling her face in his palm.

Holly felt her watch buzz.

"Ignore it," Jack said, feeling her pull away. His eyes were fixed on hers. He pulled her closer in his arms, as if not wanting to let her go. His hands were firm. Unrelenting.

Her breath quickened at his touch. Did he want this?

They had been friends for so long. Never once crossing this boundary. Not daring to go from friends, strictly friends, but to *something* more.

Jack was a good man. He was more caring than any other man in her life and he listened to what she said, like really listened. He always remembered when she was struggling with something. And then he did *this*. He had created a rose just for her. He had built a whole damn greenhouse just for her.

She *wanted* this. She wanted *him*. More than she had ever wanted somebody before. She searched his eyes.

But then she remembered the cottage, and the three rooms.

She didn't want to leave her town, her home, her neighbors. She didn't want to live in the middle of nowhere, even if it was close to the town. She liked her neighbors.

Even as nosy as they were. Hell, she didn't even know if she wanted kids. Not after losing her mom and the pain and loneliness she felt. She didn't know if she could be the source of that anguish for a child of her own. And Jack deserved a wife who wanted the same things as her.

She couldn't do this. She couldn't put herself or Jack through that. Especially when it came at the risk of losing Jack forever if things went poorly.

Her watch buzzed again. Her heart broke a little as she forced her gaze down, turning her face away from Jack. She pulled away.

Jack let her go. He turned, breathing out a loud breath and raking a hand through his golden blond hair.

Holly clicked on the watch screen button, illuminating the screen. She had missed two text messages.

> SIMON
>
> (S) Hey beautiful, I managed to change the reservation to 7 PM. Looking forward to seeing you.

What time was it? She clicked back to show the time.

> 5:55 PM

"Shit," she said. It would take at least an hour to get back to Coal River and she still had to change and get ready. She was still in the outfit she wore during work and the all black outfit wasn't exactly fit for a nice restaurant like Simon had planned.

"What's wrong?" Jack asked, frowning, noticing her panicking.

"I've got to go. I have a date with Simon, and I am running very late." She said, fiddling with her ring on her finger. Jack went stiff as soon as he heard Simon's name.

"Right. Simon." He said the name harshly. But Jack's

expression soon changed back to his normal face. He turned, guiding her back to the entrance of the greenhouse. He pulled her jacket off of the rack and held it open for her to put her arms in. His hands brushed her shoulders as he did. Every time he touched her it was like a bolt of lighting hit her and she jumped.

She missed the feeling of his hands and the way that he had looked at her but she pushed those feelings aside. Holly felt more confused than ever. He held the door for her as a shock of cold air hit her. She already missed the warmth of the greenhouse and the feeling of being held by Jack, but she forced one foot in front of the other to make their way back to Jack's cabin.

Heavy snow had fallen by the time they had left the greenhouse, which made their way back to the cabin more difficult than their way in and they had to wade through the forest as the path was almost completely swallowed by a freshly fallen blanket of snow. The snow was heavy on her boots as she pushed it out the way with each step. And more snow was still falling, covering their tracks as they went. Snowflakes clung to her hair and eyelashes. She tried to blink them away but more fell replacing the ones she had blinked away.

As they reached the cabin, Jack moved ahead of her, brushing snow off of the stoop of the cabin as he opened the door.

"It's really coming down," Holly said, biting her lip as she entered the warmth of the cabin once more. She looked out the large window out onto the lake. The snow was falling so thickly that they could barely see the lake although it was only a few feet from the cabin. The air outside was an almost blue color, with the snow now covering the light of the sun as it set.

"Hol, I don't know if you should be driving in this

weather," Jack said, moving next to her and looking at his phone. "Weather station says that a big snowstorm is rolling in and the road out is already looking covered."

No. This couldn't be happening.

"It can't be that bad," Holly said, moving out to look at where the cars were parked. Her little car was completely covered with what seemed like a foot of snow. How was that even possible? She had only been parked for not that long. Holly covered her hands with her eyes.

"Seriously, Hol, I'm not going to let you drive out there." Holly swung around to look at Jack.

"Let?" She narrowed her eyes at him. What did he mean let? She wasn't his to *let* her do anything.

"You almost crashed on your way in when it had barely begun snowing." He leveled her with his gaze and she knew that he wasn't going to give this up. She looked out of the window at the cars. The road had already been covered with a thick layer of snow, covering the tire tracks she had made while driving in. He was probably right.

"Stay the night, Hol. I'll drive your car into town tomorrow after the plows come through and clear the roads. I'll get dad to drive me back." He pleaded with Holly, being gentle with her as if saying the wrong thing would get her to break.

She opened up the weather app on her phone to check it herself. *Shit*. He was right. There was an extreme weather warning at the top of the app. She looked outside again as if to will the snow to not exist. But alas, it was still there, bright and white as ever as if mocking her. But she could do this. Couldn't she?

Holly gripped the door handle, willing herself to open the door, jump in her car and drive back into town. But her arms still hurt from her gripping the steering wheel so hard while driving down here. And she didn't have the right tires for this kind of weather. That and she was now freezing cold and her tights were now soaked from the track back from the greenhouse. The drive would be miserable. And knowing her, she'd probably catch a cold or worse, she'd crash her car and end up in the lake. Holly gripped the handle hard, her knuckles turning white.

"You did this on purpose." Holly snapped her head at Jack, accusingly, letting go of the door handle.

"I made a snow storm appear? I can do many things, but control of the weather is not one of them."

Holly let out an audible noise of frustration as she took off her Jacket and boots in defeat. The cabin creaked as wind blew against the wooden walls. Then a pop sound and the lights went out. Holly let out a squeak and grabbed ahold of Jack's arm.

"What now?"

✳

*V*isible annoyance was painted on Holly's face as she shifted through the lettered tiles in front of her. She picked up a 'J' tile between her fingers and twiddled it.

"Shouldn't you have a generator living all the way out here? Isn't that the whole point of living *off grid?*" she said, putting the 'J' down and moving around a few letters on her tile rack.

Jack chuckled at her obvious annoyance at everything that had to do with the cabin, as if the building itself was her enemy.

"This place isn't that far out from civilization. We're connected to the county power grid." Jack leaned back onto the base of the couch, and raised his eyebrow.

The two were sitting on the floor of the loft in front of a low wooden coffee table. They were surrounded by mismatched candles in glass cups, saucers and anything else non-flammable.

Holly squinted at her remaining letter tiles. The cabin

was only illuminated by moonlight, the warm flicker of candles, and a fire that burned low.

Jack took a sip of a beer, then placed it on the table as Holly put five letters on the scrabble board.

"JUNKY. Fifteen points." She grinned, slapping the table.

Jack considered her points, looking down at his own tile wrack.

Holly grabbed the velvet bag of letters to refill her own. She frowned at the letters she pulled. *Junky* was right. What garbage.

Holly rubbed her hands up and down her arms, trying to think of different words that contained the jumble of consonants she had pulled.

Jack looked over at her. The wrinkles between his brow deepened. With the power out, cold started to seep into the cabin. Jack fiddled with a tile in his fingers, grabbing a few and attaching it to her Y tile on the board. ZIPPY.

"Twenty one points." He stood as Holly's mouth hung open. She narrowed her eyes at him. He *always* won scrabble.

"Every time." She muttered under her breath.

"Maybe if you read more you'd know more words." He grabbed a log beside the fireplace and tossed it onto the fire. The log crackled as the low flame licked up the side of it. The flame burned brighter.

She gave him an exaggerated look of offense, as he disappeared down the stairs. She would have been offended, but Jack was the best read person she knew. Stacks of books were even piled up around them, not yet having a home in the cabin.

Holly pulled up the sleeves once more on the oversized hoodie that Jack had given her when she decided to stay. Her black dress and tights she was wearing had been completely soaked by the snow from their trek back from the greenhouse and she had started to shiver.

He hadn't hesitated to grab a red hoodie with big letters spelling out STANFORD UNIVERSITY on the front, and a pair of matching sweatpants for her to wear. She had to roll down everything for it to fit her. The rim of the pants were rolled and pulled tight with the drawstring, the legs were rolled up to her calves, and the hoodie sleeves were rolled up to her midarm, but they didn't want to stay there. The clothing was soft and warm and if she breathed deeply it smelled of Jack.

Holly glared at the letters in front of her. She had a few options, but they were all crap. She chewed on her lip, picked up one tile and moved it to the last slot on the tile rack.

Jack came back up the stairs with a kettle, a canister, and a bag of marshmallows in his hands. He placed the kettle on the fire using a small hook that was set in the hearth, and lifted the jar to show Holly what he was holding.

"Hot chocolate. To keep you warm."

Holly grinned back.

"You know the way to a girl's heart," she said, moving so that she was sitting on her knees. She reached to grab a marshmallow and popped one in her mouth. She relished the soft chewiness, then went to grab another one when Jack swatted her hand.

"Those are for the hot chocolate."

She childishly stuck out her bottom lip at him and he rolled his eyes in response.

"Last one before drinks." He stuck up a single finger.

She nodded enthusiastically and caught the marshmallow he tossed her way, stuffing it in her mouth. They sat in a comfortable silence, both watching the flickering flames of the fire that danced between the logs. Holly brought her knees up between her chin.

Jack looked at Holly, who was peering at the tiles with a far off look, giving no indication of finding another word.

The game seemed to be over. At least for tonight. He grabbed a blanket from off the couch and pulled it over Holly's shoulders before coming to sit next to her.

Holly leaned onto his shoulder, warming herself with his body heat. They sat there for a moment just listening to the crackles of the fire and the whistle of the wind and snow pressing against the cabin walls. Holly finally gave a hum and grabbed Jack's hand, turning it over and tracing the lines on his palm.

"What are you doing?" Jack said, and she could tell he was resisting the urge to pull his hand back.

"Shhh," Holly said, grabbing his other hand and tracing those lines as well with her index finger.

A shiver went through Jack. His hands were warm in hers.

She brushed her fingers over the rough mounds of his palms. A worker's hands. They were almost comically large.

"I'm reading your palm. Rowena is teaching me."

"Rowena taught you what?" Jack responded sarcastically, his eyes narrowed in suspicion. Jack had never warmed to Rowena. They had all gone to high school together at the one high school in town. One fateful lunch period when he and Rowena had gotten in some fight about nobody can remember about what now, a frog had jumped out Jack's lunch kit. He was convinced that she had something to do with it.

Jack didn't look the type, but he was strangely superstitious. Ever since then he was convinced the rumor that her family were descendants of the town witches was true. There were some things that you just didn't mess with, according to him.

What Jack didn't know, and what Holly had promised she would never tell, is that Holly and Rowena had conspired to put the frog in Jack's lunch kit the period prior. But Ro enjoyed the power she held in that mystery. She didn't mind people thinking she had supernatural powers.

"I'm reading your palms," Holly repeated, tracing a line that went through the center of his hand.

"This is your life line." She hovered over a wrinkle, pressing her thumb down gently, and inspecting it closely.

"Here you can see that you're had some stress in your... mid twenties. That might be the child uncle and aunt... thing." Jack gave a huff of a laugh.

"Or it could just be a line." Jack said and Holly shushed him.

She pressed down where small wrinkles intersected the life line. His eyes crinkled. She knew that he was humoring her. She traced over another that was underneath the first.

"This is your head line." Holly said, inspecting the line closely.

"I think this one is telling me that you're a good problem solver and a person who is considerate of others."

Finally, with her thumb, she traced over one wrinkle in his hand that began by his pinky.

"And this is your heart line." She held her thumb over this line, looking up at Jack with his hands cradled in his.

He froze as their eyes met. He sucked in a quick breath and folded his hands over hers. They hadn't talked about or acknowledged the embrace in the greenhouse. Both of them had ignored it. Not mentioning it since. The moment had broken and they had pretended that it hadn't happened. Holly was half convinced that he hadn't been about to kiss her, but as she looked in his eyes now her mouth went a bit dry.

She could see desire in his gaze. Her heart quickened.

The kettle hung on the fire screeched. Both of them jumped a little.

Jack pulled his hands out of hers. He let out a shaky

breath, raking his hands through his blonde hair. A frown deepened on his face. He leaned over and grabbed a cloth next to the fire and pulled the screaming kettle from the flame. He poured the hot water into two enamel coated metal mugs and scooped some hot chocolate mix into the mugs.

Jack sighed loudly and walked over to a cabinet that was built into the wall. The fine oak veneer shined with quality craftsmanship. He pulled out a small flask and waved it at her. She nodded and he poured a little in each mug. He popped a few marshmallows into each cup before handing one to Holly.

She muttered a thanks before taking it into her hands. The mug was warm but not overly hot against her hands. She placed the bottom of the mug on the table, and blew on the top. Jack did the same and they both faced forward towards the fire. She was so confused as to what to do or what to say.

She took a small sip of the hot cocoa. The cocoa was warm as it slid down her throat, with a slight sting of alcohol hitting her palette. Holly couldn't help but think of the fortune Rowena had given her.

Rowena had a knack for being eerily accurate with her gifts. After all, she had foretold her doomed relationship with Benji. Holly looked over at Jack. Jack and Benji couldn't be more different. Benji was the big city type. The type that carried his job as more important than anything, or anyone else. He was in love with working. More committed to his relationship to his employment, making money, having fancy cars, and living in a big apartment downtown than he was to her. He hated coming to Coal River. And he made it abundantly clear about that.

You will find your great love this year.

What did that even mean? She was currently going on dates with Simon, and she had met him this year. So two points for him there? But she had a hard time believing that it meant Simon. Simon was a wonderful man. Charming. Attentive. But she didn't have a spark with him. There was no magic feeling when you went on a date with somebody you really liked. He didn't make her pulse race or give her butterflies. But her made her feel secure in his attraction to her.

She took another sip of her cocoa and snuck a peek in at Jack. She caught his eye and snapped her gaze back to the fire. Her cheeks went hot and she thought for a moment she might be too close to the fire. She buried her nose in the blanket that was wrapped around her.

"This place is nice," she conceded. "Cursed. But nice." She paused. "I didn't mean what I said earlier."

"I know," he said quietly.

"Cursed?" He gave her a small smirk. "But I haven't even introduced you to the ghost of the man who built this place." A chill went through her spine. He knew she hated ghosts.

"You're not serious," she said, wrapping the blanket tighter around her and looking out into the cabin fearfully. The rest of the cabin was in pitch darkness, with each nook and cranny now seeming suspicious to her. The wind groaned against the walls as if noticing her fear, and she wondered if it wasn't her imagination that the fire seemed to grow dimmer.

"No." He grinned back at her, and she playfully nudged him with her shoulder.

"You shouldn't kid about those things. One day a ghost will show up here and you'll be sorry."

"I don't think that's possible." He raised one eyebrow at her, leveling her with a look. Then he turned to look out at the cabin as well and a small smile entered his face.

"And if there was a ghost, it would be a good ghost. This place has too many good memories to attract a bad one."

Holly gave a small noise.

"I still can't believe you did all of this," she said. "You sure you can't fix the roof?" She stuck her tongue out at him.

Jack huffed out a laugh in response. "I'm glad you like it. My dad thinks it was a total waste. In fact, I think he's mentioned it once or twice that I should have put my degree to work, like you. I think he's still disappointed that I didn't climb the corporate ladder. His son the handyman."

"Why didn't you?" Holly asked. They had never talked about why he had come back to Cole River. Jack had gotten a degree in engineering at a reputable school. He had received a full scholarship when he had gone off to college and everybody in town had assumed that they wouldn't see him again. That he would be one of the many young people who went off to get a degree and then made it big in corporate America.

Jack rotated the mug in his hands.

"Being in a nine to five killed me. It was soul sucking. Everybody thinks that working for a big prestigious company and working on projects with big budgets is rewarding and you have all of this power, but really you're just a cog in a machine. Sure, you're important to making the machine work, but they'll also just replace you if you break down." Jack leaned his head back onto the couch seat, looking at the ceiling of the cabin.

"And I was lonely," he said. "I missed everyone back here. My home."

Lonely. Holly understood that feeling. Jack was the kind of man who held his friends and family in such high regard. She could see why Jack didn't want that life for himself.

"I don't think you're a waste. I don't think I could have survived these few years without you," Holly said honestly. She put her hand on his.

"Thanks." Jack looked at her. Her gaze fell over her. And

she felt like he was looking at all of her. A crease formed between his eyes. He opened his mouth and closed it a few times.

"You seem, I don't know, different lately. I thought the rose would cheer you up, but…" He paused for a moment, not knowing if he should continue. "Are you okay, Hol?"

Her eyebrows rose. That took her by surprise.

Holly felt guilty at the look of concern in his eyes. She didn't want to be the cause of concern for her friends. She looked up at Jack giving him a smile that faltered on her lips. The corners of her cheeks tensed.

Was she okay? She wasn't so sure herself. She thought she had been hiding it well, however, she was sure the dark circles from countless sleepless nights were betraying her.

"Umm. I think so." She took another sip of cocoa. "Maybe." She could feel the lie on her tongue. Burning like a hot coal had been placed at the tip.

He was looking at her like he could see her, like really *see* her, stripped down bare of the smiles and cheery facade she put on every day. He wasn't buying her bullshit. Her mouth went dry and her throat felt like it was closing up.

She kept his gaze. The inner corner of her eyebrows pinching together.

"Everybody looks at me like I'm some kind of saint for buying the shop. But in reality I just feel the crushing weight of their expectations every day." She looked down at her mug and took in a deep breath. She felt Jack's hand on her shoulders as he gave her a reassuring squeeze.

"And if I fail with the flower store, if I'm not able to make this work, I know that I will have let them down. The town. Your mom." She felt her voice crack.

"They put so much of their lives into that place. We grew up there. It's a part of the town's history. I know that people won't say it, but they'll think that I have let my mom down. Her legacy."

She brought a hand up to Jack's and her eyes flicked up to meet his gaze.

"Its all I have left of her." She took a deep breath in.

"But that's not the worst part." Here it was. Here was the ugly truth of it all. The little thing in the back of her mind that she had been thinking all along but didn't want to admit to herself.

"I think part of me wants to fail." Holly hugged her knees in tight. She felt Jack squeeze her shoulder again. "Then I won't have to deal with the pressure any longer. I will have already disappointed everyone and the threat won't be looming over me any longer. And who knows, maybe my dad was right. Maybe it wasn't worth trying."

A tear escaped from Holly's eye and she let it roll down her face, not fighting the release of emotion. She acknowledged the little demon in her head, the voice that told her she wasn't cut out for her ambitions. Finally admiiting it made her feel lighter.

Holly leaned into Jack's body next to her, turning her face so it was buried in his arms. He reached an arm over so she could snuggle closer. She felt a kiss on the top of her head.

"You'll never be a disappointment to me, Holly MacIntosh." And she knew that he was speaking the truth. She breathed in deeply.

"You may be put on Mrs. Greywell's bad list, but you'll have good company."

Holly let out a laugh at that, sniffing in snot that had accumulated from crying.

The fire spit and crackled in front of them. Another log needed to be put on, but neither of them made the move to release each other and get up. Holly snuggled in closer to Jack, soaking in the comfort of his warmth.

She looked up at him and he down at her. Where she was, right now, snuggled up in his arms felt right. Like she fit perfectly where she was.

He tucked a stray strand of her golden hair behind her ear. A warmness settled in Holly's chest. Here in this cabin, just the two of them, it felt like they were the only people on earth.

Wind blew against the cabin walls, its faint creaking the only reminder of the old building it really was. Jack drew her in closer, shielding her from the drafty air. Holly reached up to Jack's face, cradling him in her hands.

Jack froze, his eyes widening for a fraction of a second. All of her attention was on how she felt in his arms, the feel of his skin against hers, and she was compelled by an irrational determination and irresistible need for him to have him closer to her.

Holly closed her eyes as she brushed her lips against his in a chaste kiss. His lips were rough and warm against hers. For a fleeting moment, everything else melted away. Jack's body went rigid then loose all at once, like a bolt of lighting had hit his body.

She pulled away, opening her eyes. Jack sat there, his face turned towards her with a furrowed brow, shock and confusion clear on his face. Her heart sunk to the bottom of her chest and a coldness set into her stomach. She had made a mistake, and had read the signals wrong.

"Jack." Her voice wavered as she tried to fix the situation. The silence between them was deafening. She tried to find the words– any words– that might make things right. Her heart pounded in her ears.

Before she could speak again Jack pulled her in closer. His lips crashed on hers. His fingers pressed into her sides with a hunger that left no room for doubt. He opened his mouth, returning the kiss with a fervor that took her breath away. She melted into him.

Jack pulled her on top of him so she straddled him. She leaned in, her body wrapping around his like a present. Holly gasped as his cool hands escaped under the hoodie she was wearing. His fingers explored the skin of her stomach, making bumps appear over her flesh. His thumbs came to graze the underside of her breasts.

He let out a groan as her fingers plunged into his hair. The strands were soft beneath her fingers and she breathed in his scent. They tugged at each other, deepening the kiss. His tongue flicked against her bottom lip, asking for access. She opened her mouth. Their rhythm in perfect synchronicity.

His hands wandered to her hips, pulling her closer to him in desperate need. A small moan came out of her lips as she ground herself against him.

The kiss was *everything*, and she poured herself into it. Years of unspoken thoughts and feelings. They moved in a familiarity she had never experienced before. They had never kissed before, but it felt like this was the first amongst thousands. They just *fit* together.

One hand slid down towards her bottom, the other still firmly planted on her hip, not letting her move an inch away from where their bodies connected. They broke apart, both breathing heavily. Jack leaned his forehead against hers, his nose touching hers.

"What are we doing?" he whispered as they breathed in heavily against each other.

❄

*H*olly awoke to her watch buzzing. She clicked the ignore button without looking at the watch. It was probably Mia, wondering where she was to open the shop. Holly, after all, had almost never gone a day unless she was severely ill where she didn't work at the shop.

Holly had fallen asleep in Jack's arms in the loft living room. The cabin had become frigid in the night. The fire beside them had dwindled into embers. The coals were mostly black with a few flicks of red.

She would have shivered if not for Jack's body wrapped around her. His large arms were under her shirt, tucked around her midsection. A scratchy blanket covered them and she wiggled a little, pulling it cover her shoulders.

Jack groaned behind her. His arm tightening on her torso, pulling her in closer. Holly would have rolled her eyes if she hadn't been so cold.

She smiled as the birds chirped in the background. The cabin was still. The storm had passed and the winds were no longer pounding against the sides of the wooden structure. All was quiet and calm.

She rotated in Jack's arms to face him. She took in his face.

He looked so peaceful as he slept, the weight of the world leaving no trace on his face, and she thought now that he looked younger. Holly lifted a hand to touch her lips with her fingers. Remembering the kiss– their first kiss. It was the best first kiss she had ever imagined a kiss to be. Something out of an old timey movie. Not that she had kissed *a lot* of people. But she had her share of first good and bad dates.

She thought back to her first kiss with Benji. At the time, she had believed him to be the love of her life. She had tried hard to mold every aspect of herself to match what she had thought he had wanted. But in the end, she still wasn't enough for him.

Their breakup was bad. Like screaming matches, throw stuff out of the window bad. Never speaking of and about him again. Three years of her life and countless nights filled with tears were lost to him. In the end she found him in their apartment with another woman. Some beautiful brunette that she recognized from one of his fancy firm parties. The kind where you get dolled up and the company throws a big party with free booze and taxi chits.

Holly had never fit in with that crowd, but for Benji's sake she put on a slinky dress that made her feel naked and put on her best charming personality. A fraud. Now she recognized that she felt like an imposter in their relationship. She had given him everything. And he took and took and took until there was nothing of herself left. Like mother, like daughter, she supposed. She put that thought aside.

She put her head against Jack's chest. Grounding herself in his heartbeat. She breathed in deeply.

Her watch buzzed again. Holly let out a sign. She wanted to stay cozy in the cabin with just Jack and her forever. But it seemed like the outside world wanted her back, and was going to hound her until she answered.

But she was determined that for once the world could wait. Her stomach gave a loud grumble. Apparently, however, her hunger could not wait.

She pried herself from Jack's arms, being gentle enough not to rouse him as she moved his arms from her torso. She had to go slowly as when she moved too quickly he would tighten his grip on her.

A shiver ran through her body when she was finally free. She rubbed her arms quickly up and down. She spotted the hoodie Jack had lent her discarded on the couch, and quickly pulled it on before heading down the stairs into the main part of the cabin.

Sun shone through the large windows. A single beam pierced the room, casting sun shadows on the interior. Outside there wasn't a cloud in the blue sky. There was no sign of the raging storm from the night before apart from the blanket of crisp white snow that covered most everything outside.

A loud click sounded through the cabin and the digital clock flickered on the stove in the kitchen.

There's the power, thank god for that, Holly thought.

She went over to the kitchen and located the coffee maker as the first order of business. She opened a few different cupboards, most of them empty and she wondered to herself how Jack could have survived with so little food in his house. She finally located a coffee filter and a large tub of ground coffee. She made busy work of putting water in the back and pressing the start button on the machine. She hummed to herself as the machine beeped in response.

Her stomach grumbled once more. She pulled open the door to the fridge, spying a carton of eggs and a half covered hunk of cheese. The fridge was almost as empty as the rest of the kitchen.

Jack really must have just moved in. Unless this was how he just lived regularly, which Holly hoped wasn't the case, but somehow she wouldn't be surprised. She inspected the cheese for mold, turning it over a few times and then grabbing a plate from the cupboard when she couldn't find a cutting board. She cut the cheese on the plate and then hummed a christmas tune as she grabbed a pan and put it onto the stove, turning the heat onto medium. Once it was hot, she cracked a few eggs onto the pan and covered it with the lid.

The coffee maker beeped and she said a little prayer as she scoured the kitchen for a mug. She knew they must be somewhere since they had the hot chocolate last night. Opening and closing each cupboard, she was about to give up her search and retrieve the mugs from last night to wash before she opened the last unsearched cupboard. There were the mugs.

She smiled to herself. Jack may have good taste in general layout, but in terms of organization, he needed help. The mugs did not belong in the cupboard by the stove, but should be by the kettle and coffee maker.

She grabbed two mugs and poured herself a cup of coffee. She sat on one of the stools that was tucked underneath the protruding lip of the island. Holly pushed air through her lips onto the hot beverage before taking a sip. The coffee was a blessing, warming every bone in her body. She took another sip.

She heard a snore from upstairs. Jack was still asleep.

She tapped the side of her coffee, looking around the cabin, which was far easier to see now that it was daylight. She could see the updates that Jack had put into the cabin. Its old bones of the hand hewn beams were exposed in the ceiling, mottled with a patina that only age could bring.

Her gaze landed on the small hallway that led to the bedrooms. She snapped her eyes away, looking back at her coffee. Wisps of steam wafted from the warm liquid.

She should *not* snoop. She should really *really* not snoop. But the area did catch her attention. What would Jack's bedroom look like? Her hopes for flannel sheets consumed her thoughts. He had glazed over the area *so* quickly during the tour of the cabin. She fiddled with the handle of the mug, running her finger over the speckled glaze.

She stood, taking a few strides towards the hall. She had to be quick or the eggs would burn.

Three doors faced each other. Her hand settled on the first handle. She turned it and peaked her head into the room. It was a small bedroom, filled to the brim with boxes and books. Some boxes were neatly stacked and labeled with things like KITCHEN ITEMS and others were half open with what she could imagine were old college textbooks. There were other piles of items that had been strewn about the room.

She got the distinct feeling that Jack had thrown a lot of the mess in here before she came over. He had *cleaned* for her– to the downfall of this particular bedroom. She quietly closed the door before opening the door directly behind the first.

The second room was slightly larger than the first. A large window centered the room. Antique curtains with little blue flowers hung above it. The walls were a white, like the rest of the cabin, but these had a small blue wallpaper border of yellow ducks and daisies at the top of the wall. A small antique wooden bassinet was in the corner of the room, covered in a heap of blankets.

This was a nursery. Originally at least. Holly wondered if

the bassinet was an heirloom piece or if it had been inherited with the home. Holly felt her chest tighten, and she closed the door.

The final door must be the bedroom. She opened the door, pausing for a moment. She had thought that she heard a bump. After a second of silence, she opened the door. This room was the largest of the three. Holly entered the room. A large king bed cut the room in two, with forest green sheets and a fluffy comforter. She was disappointed, yet again, by the lack of flannel.

She ran a hand against the sheets. They were heavenly soft. There was a small dresser lining the wall and two large windows that looked out onto a stunning view of the lake.

The door shut behind her. Holly jumped as she was met with Jack's hulking form. He leveled her with a look.

"You're snooping," Hh said, putting his hands on his hips.

"Why didn't we sleep *in here*?" she said, poking her tongue out from between her lips. She didn't bother denying it.

He was upon her in seconds, putting his hands behind her knees and flipping her onto the bed. She gave a squeak in surprise, her arms flying out to brace herself as she landed with a squish on the soft mattress.

"Because I don't think I could have you in my bed without doing this." He was on top of her, pinning her with his weight. She smiled, wrapping her legs around him. Her hands came up to his face.

"Especially seeing you in these clothes." His gaze darkened, looking at her under him. Fixing her with an undeniable gaze of desire. His hands came to her hips, his thumb playing with the waistband of the sweatpants.

Her watch buzzed again and she could see his eyes roll.

"Ignore it," he said again, not looking away from her. She nodded.

She held her arm out and he gently grasped it. He

brought his mouth up to kiss her wrist, while fiddling to undo the wrist strap. He discarded the watch on the bed. She closed her eyes, feeling only his kisses as he traveled down her arm with his mouth. She let out a little gasp as he reached a particularly sensitive spot on the underside of her arm. He brought a hand down to brush against her arm.

Holly opened her eyes and with a sigh she wrapped them around Jack.

He leaned down, looking into her eyes. His gaze was an endless stormy blue. His lips met hers.

The kiss was delicate at first, like a snowflake on a crisp winters day. This kiss was similar to their first, familiar and easy. His hands pressed into her and Holly felt her core heaten with a red-hot desire. She nipped at his lip, asking for more.

Jack deepened the kiss obligingly.

She could feel evidence of his desire between her legs. He pressed his hardness into her and she felt herself melt and go wobbly. She was thankful for being on her back and supported by the bed.

She wriggled her hips under his, desperate for some friction and he made a deep growling sound.

"God, Hol, you have no idea what you do to me. Do you?"

"I think I have some idea," she said as she reached a hand down to press against the hard bulge in his pants. She could feel him twitch under her ministrations. She slipped a hand into his pants. Her hand wrapped around the base of his member. She pumped him up and down with her thumb coming to brush against the head.

Jack groaned. Jack used two hands to pull down the sweatpants around her knees, before removing his own.

Jack searched her eyes for something that Holly couldn't guess what. His brow furrowed and his eyes dark with lust.

"Do you want this?" Jack asked, his thumb circling around her swollen bundle of nerves.

Holly nodded, arching her back, getting lost in the feeling of his fingers.

"Say it," Jack said, looking her directly in the eye and removing his thumb for a moment. Holly wined and rolled her hips forward, missing the contact.

"Yes," Holly panted. Jacked leaned over her, with one arm supporting his weight. He rubbed his head over her slit. God, she was so wet.

"Say it again." He teased her with his dick, circling at her entrance. His movements were slow and controlled and it was pissing her off.

"Stirling, I swear to god if you don't fuck me right now, I'm leaving," Holly huffed. Jack let out a chuckle, before pushing his hips forward, slipping inside of her.

A swear came out from Jack's lips as he pushed himself to his hilt. He settled there a moment there to compose himself. Holly's mouth opened in a moan as he slowly moved inside of her.

Her legs wrapped around him as the sensation built inside of her. Holly wrapped her arms around him as she spasmed. Her hips bucked and her world exploded into color. Jack went deeper. Holly called out Jack's name and all at once he came. Jack griped her hips tightly as waves of pleasure hit him. He slowed, pulling out.

"Holy shit," she breathed out as they breathed against each other.

Jack nuzzled his nose against her collarbone.

"Do you smell burning?" he asked and she shot up.

"Crap. The eggs." Holly leapt up from the bed. She grabbed some clothes and dashed out the room.

Jack was right behind her.

Reaching the stove, Holly grabbed the frying pan off of

the heat. The eggs had turned a strange shade of green. The edges of the egg, more brown than white were so burnt it met the yolk which had turned a dark shade so yellow it almost looked green. Holly fanned on top of the pan, trying to dissipate the smoke, which was billowing off the pan.

"There goes breakfast." Holly brought her hands over her face. She had completely forgotten about the eggs.

Jack scooped the fried remains into the trash bin.

He raised his eyebrow as she held up a single finger.

"I thought I saw some of these earlier when I was totally *not* snooping… ah hah." She opened the cupboard and pulled out a box of toaster strudel and waved it in the air in triumph.

"That is not breakfast." He let out a laugh.

"It may be all we can handle. Plus, I tried the healthy option earlier and it just was not meant to be," she said, motioning to the garbage can and popping two strudels in the toaster.

"You're practically made of sugar aren't you?" he said before he scooped her up in his arms and planted her on the countertop. The countertop was cold against her buttocks but at least the sweater was warm. She had neglected to grab the sweatpants before she ran from the bedroom but she felt cute. And she didn't mind the way that his gaze lingered on her legs. He planted a kiss on her forehead.

"You know that I have fresh fruit and veg in the panty, right?" he said, walking over to a carved wooden panel in the wall and pressing in. The wall popped in and then popped out, revealing baskets of fruit and vegetables. *Of course* he did.

He tossed her an apple before also grabbing a plate for the toaster strudel.

"So when can we get out of here?" Holly asked, taking a large bite out of the apple.

"Always in a rush, MacIntosh. You bored of my company already?" He gave her a cocky smirk, leaning back against the counter. His forearms flexed as he leaned back. He had to know how good he looked. Holly bit her lip.

"They always take at least a day to plough the road. It'll be a while yet before we can leave." He waggled his eyes at her and she punched him playfully in the arm.

❄

They had spent the morning and part of the afternoon playing board games in the cabin. Spending time with Jack was easy.

They soon settled in a comfortable silence. Holly scoured the piles of books in the loft and had found a paperback mystery novel that piqued her interest. She had draped herself over the couch to read it.

Jack settled in next to her, working on whittling a small piece of wood with a knife. The piece of wood was small enough to fit into his hand. It was cylindrical in shape, though not symmetrical, one side was slightly more bulbous than the other.

"What's it going to be?" Holly asked absentmindedly, turning the page of the novel.

"You'll have to wait and see," he said, flicking a piece of wood shaving at her.

She stuck her tongue out at him.

"More snow," Holly said, gesturing to the window. The day had been snowing on and off, which added inches to the already piled up snow.

Holly tapped her finger repeatedly on the back of the book. She had the distinct feeling that she was going to be stuck here for longer than she thought. Holly had never in her three years of owning the shop missed a day of work, let alone two days. And if they didn't plow the streets soon they may be stuck in this house another whole day.

"Hey," Jack said, sitting up, noticing her anxiousness. "I've got one more secret in this place that I haven't shown you. It'll help pass the time too." He offered a hand to her, giving her a reassuring smile. Holly grabbed his hand and he yanked her up off the couch. Jack led her to the large windows.

"You'll not need these," Jack said, coming up behind her and tugging up the sweater. He bent down to leave a trail of kisses on her neck. She nodded her head to the side to give him more access.

"I'm afraid that you don't know what a surprise is. You've already shown me this trick," Holly said, her voice more breathless than she had intended.

Jack huffed out a laugh. Jack slowly pulled the sweater off of her. Before pulling his own shirt off from the neck.

Holly shimmied the sweats off of her hips, enjoying how Jack paused pulling his own down to look at her.

Jack pressed her against the glass, his lips capturing hers.

She hissed into his mouth as the cold glass hit her, making goose bumps appear all over her skin.

Jack ran the palm of his hand over her breast, pulling her bra to the side, exposing her. He ran his thumb over her nipple, which puckered from his touch.

She arched her back, leaning into his touch.

Jack's eyes glazed over as he lazily played with her. Jack leaned in and captured her nipple in his mouth, his body flush against her. Holly was caught between the cold glass on her back and his warm body pressed against her front. Jacked flicked his tongue against her nipple and she was surprised she didn't come right then and there.

He let out a low groan. Releasing her breast he kissed his way up her chest. He pressed himself against her, letting her feel the harness between his legs.

"The secret is out here. Trust me, you'll enjoy it," he whispered in her ear.

Breaking away from her. Holly let out a grunt of disappointment. Her panties were soaked and the bundle of nerves as the apex of her sex was desperate for attention. Jack grabbed her hand, sliding open a clear glass door. Holly resisted.

"You want to go outside? Jack, I already saw the greenhouse. We're nearly naked and it's freezing out there," she said slowly as if she was talking to a toddler. She stuck her tongue between her teeth.

"Enough out of you." Jack turned on her, swooping to pick her up. Holly let out a squeak as he stepped outside. She tried to wriggle away, as a wave of cold air hit her skin. Jack held his grip tight as he stepped out into the snow. Blowing air out his nostrils as the snow hit his bare calves.

"You're unhinged," Holly said, clinging to Jack as he waded through the snow until he got to a round wooden cylinder with stairs leading to the top and a cushion top covering it. Holly laughed.

"Of course, you have a hot tub."

"It was the first thing I put into the place. And it's been so worth every penny," Jack grinned. "I'm going to have to put you down for a second." He nodded to the lid of the hot tub.

"No. No. No." Holly clung to Jack's chest like a koala, with both legs wrapped around his hips as he tried to put her down. She was already starting to freeze being nearly naked and she absolutely hated the stinging feeling of snow on her flesh if she touched the snow and went into the hot water.

"That works too," Jack chuckled. With both hands free, he quickly flipped the lid of the tub and used his foot to brush clear one of the steps to the hot tub. Holly gingerly put a foot down on the step. She could feel the warm humid air of the hot tub.

She looked down.

"I don't have another set of underwear here," she said, hesitating.

"Who said you'll need those later?" He wagged his eyebrows at her. Holly let out a laugh. But he was right. She stepped a foot into the hot water. Jack was right behind her, with a hand placed on her lower back.

Holly felt her whole body relax in a way it hadn't in months as she sunk into the water. She hadn't realized how much tension she was holding in her body. There was a ledge a few feet into the water that was meant for sitting, but Jack pulled her into his lap before she got a chance to sit.

Jack's hands were on her shoulders as soon as she was seated comfortably on him. Holly groaned as he used his hands to knead a particularly stuck spot on her back. His fingers were strong and rough in all the best ways.

She leaned forward and tilted her neck to the right.

"Yes," she said, unconsciously letting out another guttural sound.

Jack chuckled at her noises and she could feel his chest vibrate behind her. His movements slowed and she felt his lips meet her neck where his hands had just been.

Holly went still, enjoying the sweetness of the kiss. She brought one hand to his head, running a hand through his impossibly soft hair. She Had paid good money to get her hair half as soft as his. She made a mental note to snoop in his bathroom later and discover his secrets.

Jack brought a hand up to brush down the underside of her arm and all thoughts of shampoo left Holly's mind. With a single movement, Jack unfastened her bra and discarded it into the tub.

Holly gave a small huff of protest.

"You're fishing that out later."

Jack just mumbled in response. Still facing outward on

top of him, he brought one hand to cup her breast, the other making slow circles on her stomach. Torturously slow.

The hand on her breast came up, massaging it with the palm on his hand. He tweaked her nipple, pulling at it gently. Rolling it between his fingers. The other hand moved from her stomach, down her leg until it met her knees. He gently pushed her knees outward, spreading her legs. Holly gave way, allowing herself to be manipulated by him.

Holly would normally be nervous being exposed outdoors and in such a lewd position, but here, in the middle of nowhere with nothing but trees for company, she let herself relax. Sinking into the feeling of his hands on her body and his mouth teasing her neck.

Jack ran his fingers from the tip of her knee down to the cusp of her inner thigh. His fingers pressed into the fabric of her panties, lazily circling through the fabric where her clit was. Though her panties were underwater, she could feel how wet she was. Holly sucked in a breath as he pulled her panties to the side. He nibbled her neck and she let out a moan.

A single finger circled the outside of her sex as his thumb came down on her sensitive clit. Jack tweaked her nipple as a finger parted her folds and entered her with his finger. Holly cried out in ecstasy, unable to keep herself quiet as he pumped his finger in and out. Every nerve in her body was on fire and attuned to every motion of his touch. The water was hot, his fingers were hot, her core was hot.

Holly writhed in his lap but he held her steady as the feeling grew in her. Jack entered a second finger into her, stretching her, curling them inside of her. Her hips bucked against his fingers as she rode him, chasing that feeling building in her core. Holly cried out as an orgasm ripped through her. Her entire body shook.

Jack's fingers slowed as she rode the high. He kissed her

neck gently, removing them as her head lolled back to rest on his chest. Holly could practically feel the smug look on his face as he had just given her the best orgasm of her life and he knew it.

✳

Holly wrung her hair out in the towel. The sun had set by the time they had gotten out of the hot tub.

Holly had taken a nice long shower after they had returned to the cabin. She took a deep breath in. She could smell something delicious being cooked.

Jack had laid out one of his t-shirts and an old pair of running shorts on the bed for her.

Holly had spotted her bra and panties which were drying on the radiator. She went over and touched the fabric. They were still a little too damp to put on. Holly shrugged as she decided to go without, and she quickly put the clothing on before a chill set in.

Holly picked up her watch, clicking the side button to turn it on. Holly let out a sigh.

13 missed messages

She wanted to avoid the real world, but the real world just wouldn't let her go. An eerie groan sounded outside of the cabin. It sounded like a monster moaning into the night. Holly stuck her head out the door, looking at Jack with her eyes wide. She knew a forest this quiet had to be haunted.

"Those are the snow plows starting," Jack explained as cracked an egg and plopped it into a pan on the stove.

"Oh," Holly replied, feeling weirdly sad about it. She had conflicting feelings about hearing the news that their little getaway was about to be interrupted. The real world was crashing their party. She had expected to feel a sense of relief that they could drive back into town. The feeling, however, was notably absent. She looked at her watch again, staring at the messages, before deciding to place it on the nightstand unread. She could get a few more hours in before returning to reality.

Holly joined Jack in the kitchen. Jack was humming *O Holy Night* and stirring a sauce that smelled amazing on the stove.

Holly her fingers through her long blonde hair. It was going to take forever for it to air dry and there was definitely no hair dryer to be found in this domicile. She would know. She checked. Jack turned to see her as she entered the kitchen. He waved to a bottle of wine that sat on the edge of the counter and two glasses that were already filled.

Holly picked up the bottle, humming in approval.

"Pinot noir. Did you know that was my favorite or was that just a guess?" Jack tapped on the side of his nose in response.

Holly took a sip of the wine, letting the liquid slide down her throat and a soft warmness entered her belly. Holly looked at Jack. He wandered around the kitchen with ease. He seemed totally in his element.

"A true man of mystery," Holly muttered into her glass of wine, leaning back in the chair.

"What?"

"I said I didn't know you could cook."

Jack hummed in response, throwing a kitchen towel over his shoulder. Jack grabbed two plates from the cupboard and plated a scoop of pasta on each, then added a leaf of parsley to garnish each plate.

"Pasta carbonara." Jack brought a plate over to the table, where he had lit a small candle. He pulled out a chair for Holly before sitting at the chair opposite. Little pieces of yellow pasta were piled in the middle of the plate and covered in a deliciously creamy sauce. Little pieces of pancetta glistened.

"Is this homemade pasta?" Holly poked one of the pieces. They were non uniform in shape and had a satisfying bounce as she pushed it. Holly took a bite. Creamy. Zingy. And a little salty. Holly melted. Delicious. She let out a noise of satisfaction.

Jack smiled in response, happy to see that she was enjoying the meal.

As they ate the meal they settled into an easy conversation.

Jack looked at her with a spark in his eye that she had never seen before.

She wondered if it had always been there and she had never noticed. He looked at her like she was the most precious thing he had ever set his eyes upon. A seed of happiness sat low in her stomach. She felt afraid to look at that seed too closely, lest it grew and overwhelmed her. She had never felt this type of compatibility with anybody before, and it frightened her.

Holly took another sip of wine, pushing down those thoughts as Jack got up from the table and walked over to the record player that sat on a small table at the edge of the room.

He opened a drawer filled with records. And selected one with a matte black album cover. He slid the record out of the cover and placed it on the player. He flicked a switch that started to turn the record and the stylus moved over to make contact.

A bluesy voice rang out from the speakers. The song was slow and sultry. Jack extended a hand to her.

"Dance with me." He said.

Holly stood and joined him in the middle of the room. Holly placed her hands in his, and he pulled her close. They fell in step with each other and Holly pressed her head against his chest. Holly let herself be led in the dance as the music swelled and fell. They swayed in the candle light.

What were they doing? He had asked her that after their first kiss. A sinking feeling entered Holly's gut as she realized that she was falling for him.

FOURTEEN DAYS UNTIL CHRISTMAS

❄

*H*olly woke alone, wrapped in a comforter. She rubbed her eyes, picking at the small pebbles of sleep that were stuck in the corners of her eyes. She lay there in bed, not wanting to get out and face the world quite yet. The plows had come through late last night. The roads were clear into town now. She snuggled further into the covers, covering her head with the blankets.

She knew it wasn't possible, but what she would give for one more day in the cabin. Looking back to when she first found out she had to stay, she would have done anything to get back into town right away, but she had gotten accustomed to life with Jack.

She saw him almost every other day in town, but this was different. And that terrified and excited her. It was like coming home in a way she had never experienced before.

The smell of bacon and eggs floated in the air. Jack must have started to make them breakfast. Her stomach let out a low grumble of protest at her staying in bed.

"Traitor," she whispered to her stomach, throwing off the covers and stretching her arms out. She was wearing only the old t-shirt that Jack had laid out for her the day previous. The shirt covered her ass, so she figured it would be good enough for breakfast.

Holly went to the bathroom first, grabbing Jack's deodorant and giving it a sniff. *Pine.* She shrugged before lifting the shirt and applying it. She wouldn't mind smelling like Jack for a little bit longer.

Holly trodded out of the bedroom and into the kitchen, following the smell of breakfast.

Jack turned to look at her as she entered, giving her one of those dazzling smiles that made her heart stop.

"I could get used to this." She made a cooking motion, before hoping up on the counter. The cool stone of the countertop made a shiver go down her spine as she leaned back. Jack handed her a cup of coffee and she took a sip.

"I bet you could. I've seen the way you eat." He scooped out a small portion of egg from the frying pan and brought it to Holly's mouth.

"What do you think? Does it need salt?" Holly chewed the piece, before bringing her hands up in a little pinch motion. Jack grabbed a canister labeled 'salt' and tossed a pinch of the white granules in the pan before stirring. He plated two servings of the eggs and placed a few strips of bacon on each plate.

Holly pouted, opening her mouth for another serving. Jack chuckled and compiled, positioning himself between her legs before bringing a spoonful of eggs to her mouth. Holly gave a hum of approval. Jack's hands settled onto the top of her thigh, his fingers drawing lazy circles that made her squirm.

Jack's phone rang in his pocket.

"Now who should ignore it," she teased as he pulled the phone out his pocket. He glanced down at the phone for a second to see who was calling.

He frowned.

"It's Rowena," he said, before breaking away to answer it. Holly's eyebrows rose. *Ro? What was she doing phoning Jack during this time of the morning?* She was surprised that Ro was up this early. What could she want from Jack?

"Hey Ro," he said, turning away from Holly. Holly felt a surge of what she could only describe as jealousy rise within her chest. She pushed it back down. To be jealous of Rowena calling Jack was the most ridiculous thing. Holly had been ignoring all text messages from her own phone, so Ro was likely just trying to get a hold of her.

She didn't like that feeling of being out of control of her feelings. Of her heart. To be out of control would be to be vulnerable, and they hadn't even had a chance to have a conversation about what *this* was anyways.

"Yeah, she's with me." He looked back in her direction. She could hear a hint of worry in Jack's voice. A bad feeling settled in her stomach.

He nodded a few times before Jack went silent and Holly tried to strain to hear the conversation.

"We'll be right there. Thanks for calling, Ro." Jack hung up the phone but stayed with his back turned from her. He brought a hand up to rake through his hair, before turning around. A deep frown had settled on his face and Holly sucked a breath in.

Her stomach turned to ice. She recognized the look on his face. It was a look combined with pity and hesitation. The same look that the doctors gave her when her mom was sick and they didn't want to give her the news that her mother's organs were failing.

"Just tell me," she said, the corners of her mouth tugging downward and all remnants of a smile wiped off her face.

Jack was silent for a few seconds longer.

"The store roof caved in."

❄

Holly's fingers felt numb. Her feet felt numb. Her tongue felt numb. She was numb.

She stared out the window of Jack's truck as they traveled back down the gravel road towards Coal River. She vaguely remembered Jack putting her coat on her. She had stood outside, not noticing the snow fall on her eyelashes as Jack had affixed snow chains to the tires of his truck. He had tucked her in the cab, letting her use his hand as leverage to get inside.

They drove in silence, Jack not pushing her to make conversation.

She felt like she was in a dream, like she was sleepwalking, like this was a nightmare. She ran through all of the scenarios of what could have happened in her head, each one worse than the last. Jack drove straight to the shop as they had gotten into town.

The shop looked the same from the exterior. The historical saloon facade was still standing, its square corners as square as ever. The only hint that anything was wrong was the yellow and black hazard tape that was criss crossed against the front door. The OPEN sign was hanging in the front door and Holly's heart sank.

She hoped to god that Mia or Finley hadn't been inside when it had happened. She didn't know what she would do if anybody had been injured due to the neglected state of the roof.

An older man with a large white beard stood outside in a red hard hat and notepad. Holly assumed that was the structural engineer. The truck rolled to a stop and Holly leaped out the car. The man looked up, eyes wide, as she blurted out a string of questions about what happened, *how* could this have happened, and if everyone was okay. The man held his hands out in surprise.

Jacked walked up behind her, putting a hand behind her back.

She breathed in and out, her nostrils flared.

Holly's head snapped up as the door to the shop swung open. Rowena and Mia emerged from the shop, both with the same grim looks on their face as was mirrored by Holly. She swung her arms around them both, bringing them into a tight hug. They embraced her back.

"What happened?" Holly asked, squeezing Mia.

"I was in the front this morning, working on the display and there was this crash, and then there was a huge puff of snow and the was sun shining in through the ceiling. I'm so sorry Holly, there was nothing I could do." Mia wiped a tear from her face. Holly shook her head.

"I tried calling you when it happened, but I couldn't reach you. Where were you?" Mia tried to not look it, but she was mad.

Holly's mouth went dry. Holly couldn't say anything to make it better. It *was* her fault. She knew she should have called the structural engineer earlier. She should have known that something was wrong. But she thought she had more time. She knew it was bad but instead she had been selfish. She wanted to ignore it. Because by ignoring it she wouldn't have to admit that she was struggling to make it. She was the *owner*. She should be able to handle this. She should have been here, with the shop, with her first priority instead of...

Jack walked over with the engineer.

"Hi, I'm Christopher. Your husband and I spoke on the phone" The older man reached a hand out to introduce himself and Holly took his hand in hers. He gave it a firm shake.

Holly had found Christopher online and had been emailing back and forth with him. *True North Structures.*

Jack had taken the number from her and phoned the engineer as soon as he had told her what had happened at the shop. Holly avoided Jack's gaze. Not wanting to deal with the feelings rising in her. She had to focus on the task at hand. She had to focus on the shop.

"He's not my husband," Holly said flatly.

Rowena shot a look between Holly and Jack. She looked at Holly as if to ask what was going on there and why was Holly with Jack early in the morning. Her dark eyes shot through Holly in the way they always did when she could tell that Holly was hiding something from her.

A small crowd of townsfolk had gathered outside and were talking to each other about the shop.

Holly tried not to notice if she recognized anybody. Holly let Mia know she could go home and rest. The woman looked shaken up, and Holly recognized that her friend needed to be home. She tried to assure her that she did everything right, but she wasn't convinced of her own behavior. She had let her staff down. She hadn't been there for them in their time of need and now she had to amends for that fact.

They entered the shop. Finley was inside waiting for them. Everything in the shop was covered in a fine dusting of snow. Sun shone through the back of the shop, where the store room was located and Holly could see a large lump of snow and debris that had sunken in. Most of the store thankfully looked unchanged, apart from the dust, debris and snow that had made its way in.

Christopher stopped them before they entered any further.

"Everybody grab one," he said, motioning to a large and very lumpy sack he had placed by the front door.

Jack reached into the sack.

"Ho. Ho. Ho." He waved around a cherry red hard hat he had pulled out that had the Christmas saying printed on it in cursive red letters. He passed it to Rowena who looked at it distastefully, before passing it on to Mia muttering to herself something about red not being her color.

Rowena grabbed the bag for herself, which clattered together as she fished out a deep forest green hat that had a few pine trees printed on it instead. She twisted her long black hair into a braid before placing the hat on her head.

Jack grabbed the sack back, rifled through it and passed Holly a light blue hat that had snowflakes printed on the side before he found one for himself. He had to try on a few that didn't quite fit his head before he settled on a deep blue hat.

"Seriously," Rowena said, hiding a snicker, "Mistletoe?"

Two sprigs of mistletoe were printed on the side of the hat. Jack's ears went a little red, not realizing what was on the hat he had put on.

"Why Ro? I didn't know you were angling for a kiss," Finley said, wagging his eyebrows at her and holding a hand out for Jack to hand him the helmet.

"Okay Casanova," Ro stuck her tongue out at Finley.

"Now that everyone has a hat, please stay in the front of the shop while I complete my assessment. It looks like the damage occurred exclusively to the addition of the shop, and this section is stable still. I will let you know when I have completed my work," he said gruffly.

The man's face was flushed with what looked like permanent redness over his cheeks and nose, which gave him a much more jolly appearance than what his personality showed. Christopher took a moment to explain what they could expect before the man turned. A serious look was on his face as he walked towards the worst damaged area of the shop.

Holly took in the shop. The power had been turned off until the inspector could clear it to be turned on again. The shop was still. Silent. Apart from Finley and Rowena who had both grabbed brooms and were beginning to sweep up the store.

It had began to snow outside. Snowflakes entered the shop through the hole in the roof. They glittered like diamonds as they fell through the beams of light that lit up the shop. With everything covered in a thick layer of snow and soot, Holly couldn't help but think the shop looked like a tomb. The tables and chairs were the gravestones and the flower bouquets were there in memoriam of a time lost.

Jack had gone to the far side of the shop and was talking about something to Christopher. They were both pointing at some part of the structure of the roof. The shape of the roof was twisted and fractured. Large wooden beams were splintered and broken.

Holly's watch buzzed. Her father's name flashed on the screen. She fumbled in her pocket trying to find her phone before the call ended.

"Hello?" she said after sliding the answer button.

"Hi. I missed your message." Her dad was short and to the point.

"That's okay. I was just in the City and I figured you might want to visit. I know it was last minute."

"It was. My schedule was busy that day. You know that with work I need to have these things scheduled. It's a very busy time."

"Right," Holly responded after a pause. She had heard this excuse before. It was never not a busy time at work with her father. She was just not a priority to him.

A loud crash sounded followed by a curse at the end of the shop.

"Are you at a construction site?" Her father sounded annoyed at the interruption.

"Oh no. I'm just at the shop, there was a leak in the roof and–"

"The leak in the store room?" Her father interrupted her.

Holly was stunned. How did he know where the leak was?

"That's been there for years. I told your mother many times that she needed to get that fixed. But that woman would just never listen to me—"

Holly's mouth hung open. She felt like a bucket of ice had been poured over her head. Her mother had known about the leak and had done nothing about it. Did paulette know about it? How she been screwed from the beginning on this business. Holly felt betrayed. She felt a red hot anger start to bubble in the pit of her stomach. She had been abandoned and betrayed by every person in her life.

"You know dad, it's really not a good time for me." She hung up the phone on him. Holly paced at the front of the store.

She remembered the days that followed after her father had left her and her mother. It was a painful memory. More than once she had picked her mother off the floor in moments of pure grief. After those *wobles*, as Paulette called them, her mother wouldn't get out of bed for a few days. There was one night in particular, the first wedding anniversary after the divorce, that stuck in her mind as she looked at Jack now.

Holly had gone to the shop after school to only discover that her mother had not shown up that day. Paulette didn't seem surprised by the absence. She had gone home and called out for her mother, but she wasn't home. She searched all over town for her mother, and by the time Holly had given up her search and gone back home it was dark out.

Not a single light was on in their home. She didn't know it as she was a child, but her mother had drank too much and Holly had found her crying in the bathtub. She had a glass of red wine in one hand and the bottle in another. Streams of black mascara ran down her face. The bathwater was cold by the time Holly pulled her from the water.

Her mother had sobbed as she wrapped a towel around her and brought her a pair of pajamas. As she put her mother in bed, Margaret had pulled her in close. She had taken Holly's face in her hands.

"Men will take everything from you if you let them, darling. All they care about is their own hopes and dreams. They take and take and take until there is nothing left. But you won't let them, will you?" Holly had shaken her head. "No. You won't. You're my strong little rosebud. You'll make it on your own. Follow your own dreams and don't be distracted by a man. You should never need to rely on a man." She gripped Holly with an intensity that scared her.

"You're too sensitive, my girl. You wear your heart on your sleeve and you need to protect yourself. You're like your mama that way," she slurred her words. Too drunk to remember them in the morning.

She saw how her mother had withered after her father's abandonment of them, and how much joy and purpose that the shop had brought her. It was the only thing that brought back her mother's spirit. She was, in so many ways, similar to her mother. Everybody who knew her told her so.

She was doomed in some ways of repeating her mother's fate. With Benji, she already had. But Jack was different. She was sure of it. And that *terrified* her.

She had let herself fall for Jack. And yet her world was falling apart around her.

Holly grabbed a rag and busied herself with cleaning up. She was lost in thought when Ro tapped her on the shoulder.

"I think I might go out to grab everybody something to eat. Would you like me to pick you something up?" Holly shook her head.

"We won't be long." She forced out the words, she was going to break any moment now but she had to be strong. She didn't want to let this feeling of rage and betrayal consume her. She nodded at the engineer, who seemed to be wrapping up. "Why don't you meet me at home."

"Are you sure?" asked Rowena, her eyes softened with concern.

"Yeah," Holly said. Rowena looked at her like she wanted to say more. But ended up bringing her lips into a thin line, and nodded before turning to leave. The bell above the front door rang as she opened the door and left.

Holly knew that when she got home that Rowena would be grilling her on where she had been the past few nights and Holly wasn't sure if she was ready to tell. For now she needed some space to process everything.

Christopher motioned her over after a few minutes. He was tapping his clipboard rhythmically with a ballpoint pen.

Christopher explained to her that the snow from the storm created too much weight on the weakest point of the roof structure, which had already been damaged and neglected.

"There is some good news." He stroked his white beard.

Good news. Good news? What good news could come from this catastrophe?

"The damage was contained to the back portion of the store, which appears to be an addition."

Holly took an unconscious step back. That was... unexpected. She had no idea that there was an addition on the store. She had always thought that the entirety of the store was original to the old saloon. She had been told by the heritage society that it was, in fact, all original, and that she couldn't change a thing about the store because of its supposed heritage value.

Holly breathed out of her nose. Another betrayal.

"The front of the store can remain open. But the back needs to remain closed until repairs can occur."

Christopher rubbed his large belly as he walked her and Jack through the store, pointing out various different structural things that honestly went right over her head. She couldn't seem to retain any information right now. She just kept replaying it all over in her mind. The last few years. The bills. Her father telling her that her mother knew. She *knew*. All. Along.

Holly took off her hardhat as she walked to the front of the store with Jack and stuffed it in the sack. They exited the store.

Christopher said his goodbyes with a promise to be in touch with plans.

Jack wrapped his arms around Holly.

"It's all going to be okay," he said, kissing the top of her head.

"It's not. But that's okay," she said, burying her head into his chest. The cotton shirt he was wearing was soft against her cheek.

She knew what she had to do. Holly put her hands against his chest. She listened to his heart through his shirt. Her heart was screaming for her to stay here. Right here. She pulled away, looking up at him from between her lashes.

"You never got your kiss," Holly said, coming up on her tiptoes. He gave her a half smile in a question. Holly brought one hand to tap his head where the mistletoe had been located on Jack's hardhat, another wrapped around his shoulders.

Jack gave a huff of laughter. But he gave her a look.

Holly tried to keep her cool and school her face to appear

normal. She didn't want to show the emotional battle that was going on in her head.

Jack opened his mouth as if to say something but Holly tipped her head upwards and captured his lips on hers. Holly deepened it, bringing both hands around his neck. She buried her hands in his hair.

This was a kiss she wanted to remember. For it would be the last kiss that they would ever share. She tried to burn every chaste movement, every ounce of feeling into her brain.

She knew that she had to let Jack go. She couldn't risk it all for him. Something needed to change in her life, and for once, she needed to listen to her mother and prioritize herself and her dreams. Her chest felt like there was the weight of a thousand elephants on it, ripping her apart.

So she kissed him now like her life depended on it– like her heart depended on it.

ELEVEN DAYS UNTIL CHRISTMAS

❄

*I*t had been a few days since the snowstorm and this was the first time she had been out. She had stuck to her two main places. The shop and her house. She had spent a day in bed the day after the shop. She couldn't force herself to leave. Like every ounce of energy had been sucked from her. Like she was treading through water.

Her heart ached.

Jack had come to drop off her vehicle, but Holly had refused to see him. She asked Rowena to tell him that she was out. Ro had been confused, but had done what she had asked.

Ro had come to check in on her a few times since then. She hadn't asked what had happened between her and Jack. But when Holly still hadn't gotten out of bed by seven that day, Ro practically forced Holly out of bed and into the TV room with the promise of a tub of ice cream and several DVDs of their favorite holiday movies.

"Do I need to kill him?" Ro asked after movie number two.

Holly buried her head in her lap. She couldn't get the moment of them dancing in the cabin out of her head. She shook her head and groaned.

"Curse him then. I can curse him." Ro nodded as if certain that was the answer. Ro let out a squeak as Holly threw a jelly donut at her.

"No killing. No cursing." Ro narrowed her eyes at her, but took a big bite of the donut that she had fished out of the blankets in the couch.

"Jack did nothing wrong. And that's disgusting." Holly pinched her nose. She had to get him *out* of her head.

"You seem worse than when you broke things off with Jerkface. And you're the one who threw it."

Holly shot a glare at Ro. But she knew that Ro was right. She had been avoiding Jack. She knew in her head that she had to give him up, but her heart wouldn't let her do it. And so instead she had been avoiding it. In truth she had been avoiding everything. She just wanted to go back in time, but life didn't work like that and so she stayed in bed until she could muster the courage to face the world.

"I just don't have time for those things right now. I need to focus."

"You don't have time… for Jack?" Ro looked at her with skepticism. "The man's a grump but he practically worships the ground you step on."

Holly threw another donut at her, but this time Ro swung to the side and caught it in her mouth. She leveled her with a look that Holly couldn't quite take seriously as Ro still had a little bit of donut sticking out of her mouth.

"I don't want to talk about it."

"You can't avoid him forever." Holly narrowed her eyes at Ro.

"You've been talking to him."

Ro held her hands up.

"You can't blame the guy for reaching out since you've not been answering his texts. He's worried about you, Hol."

"I'm fine," she said as she looked forward. Not able to meet Ro's eyes.

"Put on the next movie," she said stubbornly. Making it clear that this was the end of the conversation.

Holly had been ignoring Jack's text messages and his phone calls. She couldn't face him. Not right now. She had to focus. She knew she wasn't being fair to him.

❄

She hadn't even been back to the shop. She had left it closed for the last few days. After days at home Ro had forced Holly to put on deodorant and real clothes and leave the house.

Holly had wandered around the town a bit before she went to the shop. She had given Mia and Finley the past few days off. The shop was technically still able to be open, but she couldn't bring herself to face the public.

As she pushed the door open the bell rang. A thick plastic sheet had been stapled to the wall in the back of the shop, closing it off from the elements. Mia and Finley had been back and had completed the tidying up. It looked as if nothing catastrophic had occurred in the shop. The only sign of anything amiss was the plastic sheet that snapped and ballooned every so often with the wind.

Holly went to the till, and ran her hands along the keys. She knew that Ro was right. She had to wake up from this slumber that she was in. Holly looked out to the store. It was just the same as when her mother and Paulette had owned it. Not much had changed. She tried to remind herself of *why* she had bought the store. What passion had burned under her when she had first opened up and tried to think about how she had slowly lost it.

She knew that something had to change. *She* had to change. She needed to find that fight in her once more. And she knew that she had to give up Jack in order to do that. The thought ached. She ached.

But her mom was right. She had let a man distract her again.

She had changed herself in the past for a man, Benji, thinking that she could change him. That he would change for her. But love wasn't enough. It is *never* enough. That was what her mom had told her over and over again as she grew up. She fought against the idea, but she shouldn't have.

Her mom hadn't let the store fall apart. She wasn't a perfect mother. There were moments of her childhood that Holly remembered with soreness, but she was a good woman, who didn't let the people around her down. Not like Holly had.

If she wasn't perfect, then she was worthless.

That was when she got the text from Simon.

> (S) I got you a spot at the
> Christmas Fair

❄

Holly had messaged him to set up a time to meet. He had taken it in stride when she said that she wasn't interested in dating. And yet, he had talked to the Christmas Fair board and gotten her a spot at the Christmas fair nonetheless.

Simon came to the table, a small chocolate croissant in tow.

"I told the organizers of your store, and the wreck that recently happened to it. You have some friends in high places it seems." Simon got straight to business. Holly appreciated that.

Once she had broken it off, Simon didn't push her. He didn't ask why or get mad. He just said okay. In fact, it appeared that he had been flirting with the barista as she spied the the woman's number written in blue ballpoint pen under the pastry as he picked it up to take a bite. Holly looked at him in question.

"One of the board members, some big wig investor type, vouched for your business. Said they had met you before and that your shop would be an invaluable addition to the fair." Simon took another bite of the pastry, wiping up the crumbs with the back of his hand.

Holly was surprised. Had Oliver recommended her shop? She hadn't heard from him since their meeting. She hadn't been sure if she should reach out to him. There wasn't much to invest in with a shop that was quite literally falling apart at its seams.

She took a sip of her hot chocolate.

The hair on the back of Holly's neck stood up as a cool breeze came blustering in from the door of the cafe. Holly got the distinct feeling that she was being watched. She looked up from her seat beside the window to see Jack, on the opposite side of the street.

He looked tired. Holly didn't break his gaze as he crossed the street in a few strides. Holly knew she couldn't avoid him forever. She was going to have to face him eventually and he wasn't going to let her run any longer.

Simon followed where she was looking as Jack entered the cafe, making a B-line for where they were sitting. It took seconds from when they had locked eyes to when he was upon her. Jack was breathing heavily as he approached.

"I need to talk to you."

"She's already occupied. Do you make it a habit to walk in on other people's dates?"

"I wasn't talking to you, bar boy."

Simon stood up. Ready to defend Holly if needed.

"Jack, please." Holly gave Simon a look, letting him know it was okay. She knew she was in the wrong in this situation anyway. She nodded at Jack, motioning to the door.

He looked at Holly with an intensity that told her that he didn't want to let her out of his sight again, lest she disappear. But he nodded and raked his hands through his hair, hair that Holly now knew how it felt between her own fingers.

Holly was torn by how much she wanted to run her hands through it again and throw herself into his arms. But that desperate feeling made her realize how much she was making the right choice. She had to steel herself now. She had to be strong in her choice to put herself first.

"I'll only be a minute," she told Simon, as she gathered her coat and followed Jack outside of the cafe. The cafe was in a quieter part of town. For a town that was normally bustling and busy, the stillness of the street unnerved her. She had nothing to distract her from the conversation she was so desperately trying to avoid.

She met Jack's eyes. He looked disheveled. A heavy feeling sat deep in her belly.

Jack was tense. His face was fixed in an unreadable expression apart from a slight furrow at his brow.

"This wasn't what you think it was. I'm not seeing Simon," Holly blurted out. She wanted to explain to Jack. She was despicable for ghosting him, but not that despicable.

"I don't care that you're with him," he spat out the last part. Holly wasn't convinced.

"I care about *you*. I haven't heard from you in a week.

You're not answering my texts or phone calls. What the hell, Hol?"

"I just can't do this, Jack," Holly said, bringing her arm up to cross them together. Jack went still.

"This?" Jack asked, his face cracked as if she had confirmed every bad thing he ever thought about himself, and Holly felt her heart break all over again.

"You mean us?"

Holly felt the cold of the air flowing over her. She had to get through this. She willed ice to fill her heart heart over.

"I just—I keep hearing my mom's voice in my head since what happened with the shop. She always said I should focus on myself, you know? That... maybe I'm better off not getting too wrapped up in anyone else."

"Your mom's always had her opinions. But what's that got to do with us?" Jack didn't raise his voice but she almost wished that he had.

It would have been easier if he had been mad at her. If he had been mad she could have felt better about what she was saying

She knew from the look on his face that his heart was breaking as much as hers. She had to do this.

"I guess I've been wondering if maybe she's right. Maybe I'm losing sight of who I am... what I need," Holly said, not able to look Jack in the eye any longer.

"Holly, you're not losing anything. You're... you're still you," he said softly, he took a step forward, but Holly took a step back.

She didn't want him to get close. She couldn't let herself slip again. She shook her head. Holly turned, but Jack caught her hand in his, not wanting to let her go. Not wanting her to slip through his fingers. Holly could see Simon stand from inside the cafe, ready to defend her if she called upon him.

"Please," Holly's voice broke, "let me leave," she said.

He released her hand as if he had been burned.

Though their hands were no longer touching, and they were no longer connected, Holly felt as if her heart was still tethered to him. And in his absence so went all sense of feeling. She turned and walked back into the cafe though her heart screamed at her to turn back round. She kept walking, one foot in front of the other.

It was *better* this way.

NINE DAYS UNTIL CHRISTMAS

❄

*H*olly held the invitation in her hand. Turning it over once and rubbing her thumb against the soft touch coating on the thick stock paper. Holly had never seen such an expensive looking invitation. It was fancier than most wedding invitations she had received over the years.

In big letters, embossed in gold, it read, "YOU'RE INVITED TO THE STARLIGHT BALL".

At the back of the invitation a number of logos were printed, including the Ridgemont Investment Company. Holly bit her lip.

"What's that?"

Holly jumped as Rowena entered the kitchen.

Rowena was in matching fuzzy pajamas that had owls in Santa hats. She gave a big yawn as she sat down at the kitchen island opposite to Holly.

Holly passed over the invitation.

"Woah. Thick paper." Ro waved the invitation about, causing the paper to make a wobble sound.

"Why were you invited to this?"

Holly brought her lips into a thin line. She grabbed the invitation back from Ro, who had placed it on the table after she picked off the gold wax seal and placed it in her pocket. She didn't respond to Ro.

"I put some coffee on," Holly said instead. Ro made an approving sound, bringing her hands into a steeple. She didn't seem to notice that Holly had evaded her question.

Holly had been thinking about when she met Oliver. He made her no promises. But Holly wasn't sure if she could trust him. In a small town, big city investors were made out to be the antithesis of everything that small town's held dear. They were the big bad wolf. But Oliver seemed like a normal person. A nice person, even. But the niceness and normalness made her all the more cautious.

Holly was sure that this invitation was a means to butter her up. She looked at it suspiciously, as if the investors had implanted a chip in that could read her thoughts.

"I'm still not selling," she whispered to the invitation.

"What?" asked Ro, who was pulling a bowl containing icing out of the fridge. Holly waved her hands at her as if to say 'nothing.'

She focused on the invitation, specifically the line about a plus one.

Ro looked at her. "Did you sleep at all last night?" she asked. Holly knew that dark circles were growing deeper by the day.

"I've got to go," she said, shoving the invitation into her bag and heading out the door.

❄

Holly's thumbs were sore from bundling up bouquets of roses and babies breath with sprigs of juniper and these little pine cones on sticks that were covered in glitter. Thank goodness for one-day shipping.

The short days of winter had brought a glow to the shop after hours. The carolers, which were a daily occurrence this close to Christmas, could be heard faintly throughout the shop.

Mia gave a big yawn. Finley tossed another finished bouquet at Mia, which smacked her in the face. Mia leveled him with a stony glare.

"We're almost wrapped up here. You both should go home and I can finish up the last few orders," Holly said as she rolled her neck out. They were all tired and she figured they could use a break before a fight broke out. The three of them had put the bouquets together for the Christmas market all day and all night. Holly hadn't stopped working. She hadn't slept much either. Purple skin darkened the underside of her eyes and the skin of her face felt cold and rough.

The fair was tomorrow and there was still a lot to do, but she couldn't ask her employees to stay so late. She knew that she would be up all hours of the night, so she may as well be preparing for the fair in the wee hours instead of being in her bed awake in the wee hours. Mia and Finley shared a look between each other.

"I don't want to hear it." Holly ignored them. She waved them away before grabbing another bushel of roses and started to prep the stems for the bouquets.

Holly had plugged in a space heater to heat the front of the store. She had propped up a large piece of plywood that she had found in the alley behind the store in the doorway that led to the damaged storeroom. It wasn't a permanent solution, but it kept the warmth in better than the plastic sheet.

As Mia and Finley were gathering their things, the bell at

the front door rang. Holly didn't look up from the bouquets she was fastening together.

She heard Ro's voice as she greeted Mia. Holly looked up as she saw Mia whispering something to Ro. Finley took the trolly filled with boxes of cookies that Ro had baked and rolled it into their freezer storage area.

Ro met her eyes. Concern was written on her face.

She walked over to where Holly was sitting. She was carrying two grocery bags stuffed with junk food. She placed the bags down unceremoniously on the table.

Mia waved at Holly as she and Finley left the store.

"Here. Food." Rowena said as she ripped open a satchel of cookies and popped one in her mouth before sitting down.

"Not hungry," Holly replied, looking down at the roses she was bundling with a piece of twine. She wasn't hungry, though she couldn't remember the last time she ate something.

Rowena leveled her with a look.

"Not hungry. Not in my twenty-eight years have I ever known you to reject a cookie. You must be bad."

Holly glared at Ro.

"Seriously though, Hol, I am worried about you. You haven't taken a break for days. You've been here for every waking moment. You leave first thing in the morning and come home late at night. Have you even been sleeping? I keep seeing the light on in your room."

"I've taken breaks. I went to the bathroom a few hours ago." Ro leveled her with a look. A bathroom break did not count as a break.

Holly hissed as a thorn pricked her already sore thumb. She put the appendage in her mouth, sucking on it. Holly tossed a pair of rose gloves to Ro, and grabbed a few stems demonstrating how to prep the stems.

Ro picked up a few roses, and began to rip off the lower

leaves on the stems, placing them in a pile for Holly to use in the next bouquets.

"I saw Lumberjack at the store today," Ro said, splitting the silence. Holly fixed her eyes on the flowers in front of her, twisting a thread around to fix them together.

"Oh."

"He looked like shit."

Holly hummed in response. She both didn't want to hear anything about Jack but also was desperate to hear if he was okay.

"If you would just tell me what happened."

"Nothing happened," Holly raised her voice, slamming down a few stems of flowers, crushing the buds. Holly cursed under her breath. Trying to salvage the crushed stems, but petals just flopped off and onto the table.

"Nothing happened. Jack didn't do anything." Ro was silent.

"So did you do something then?" Ro said tentatively, not looking up from the roses she was working on.

"Did you... compromise his innocence."

Holly shot a glare at Ro.

"You're really bad at this *'I don't want to talk about it'* thing."

"What? You can't keep me in the dark when you're out here avoiding all mention of the man, you're pretending like your best *man* friend doesn't exist, and he's out here looking like you shot his puppy... or took his favorite ax or something."

EIGHT DAYS UNTIL CHRISTMAS

✳

*T*he booth had been busy. Holly didn't have any time to think about *anything* or *anyone* but flowers and sales. The day went quickly and her cheeks hurt from keeping a smile on her face as she greeted patrons and schmoozed her way through the day. The fair was full of tourists bundled up in rabbit fur hats and long puffy jackets.

There was a buzz about the air that Holly tried to capture in herself. She wished she could bottle this feeling to put it in a bath to use later when she needed a boost.

Mia waved at a group of children who were riding on a sleigh pulled by massive brown horses. The bells that were fastened to the reins giggled as they trotted past. The sleigh master yelled at absentminded pedestrians to move out of the way.

She had to just make it through the day. And sell as much as she could. Holly kept the image of the shop in her mind when she had first seen the roof collapsed. The snow covered the inside like dust in a mausoleum.

The shop. She was doing this for the shop.

She couldn't shake this hollow feeling.

Mia and Finley were run off their feet trying to whittle down the crowd that had started to grow in front of their booth. The idea of cookies and flowers seemed like it was a hit. They had one of the busiest booths in the whole market.

Mia had made a few social posts about it. One of which went viral. Several people had mentioned that they had seen the post and had made the trip specifically to visit their booth. Holly was impressed.

She hadn't considered social media before. She thought there was too much noise already out there to actually break through and get to anybody. Especially being a shop in a small town. But she was happy to be pleasantly surprised.

Rowena gave her a grin as she left to get another box of cookies from the cooler in the shop to refill the display. Holly knew there would be a few 'I told you so' in her future.

Holly breathed out a sigh when there was finally a lull in the customers. She took a moment to herself to take a look at their sales statistics on her phone, which had been connected to their wireless point of sales software.

"Good day?" Holly's head shot up, embarrassed to be caught on her phone in front of a customer. She was met with a charming smile. It was Oliver Kilton.

He was dressed much more casually than the last time she had seen him, though still looking expensive. He was wearing a long black wool coat with matching black leather gloves.

"Oliver." She smiled at him. "Yes. Very. And I think I have you to thank for that."

"Certainly not. I just told the board about my experience with your business. The credit goes to you." Oliver leaned over to smell one of the bouquets.

A woman with curly auburn hair stepped up next to Oliver. She had an acute air of confidence about her in a way that commanded attention. The woman pointedly looked over her booth as if she was assessing its worth.

"Marla, this is Holly Macintosh. The owner of the flower shop I was talking to you about last week."

Holly felt like she was stripped down to her underthings under the scrutinizing gaze of the woman. Holly took off her glove and stuck a hand out.

"Impressive display. Novel idea." The woman looked at her for a second and then took her hand and gave it a firm shake. Holly's heart skipped a beat.

"Thank you," she said, keeping her head held high. Holly felt an immense amount of pressure to impress this woman. She stood a little taller.

"Do you do orders? Special events?" The woman said, picking up a bouquet of roses and smelling them. She made a humming noise as she placed them back on the table.

"I assume Ollie gave you my details." Holly nodded. "Call me. Let's set up a meeting." Marla picked up one of the business cards that sat on the table and turned it over before placing it in her purse. A little zing of pride shot through her. She didn't know why, but she wanted this woman's approval.

"And I'll take ten orders of these. The bundles, that is, with the cookies," she said, waving over the display. She snapped her fingers and out from somewhere behind her appeared a credit card yielding assistant.

Holly let out a quick breath as the woman then moved on to the next booth. She waved for Oliver to follow. He said a quick goodbye before following his boss.

Finley stepped up to place the orders in takeaway bags and handed them to the assistant. The woman looked overloaded as she hurried to catch up with her colleagues.

"Who was that?" Rowena asked as she put three boxes of cookies on the table. Holly opened the display case before putting on a plastic glove and placing the cookies onto each shelf. They had peanut butter chocolate cookies, Christmas tree sugar cookies, and a snickerdoodle. The last of which seemed to be the favorite.

"Uh nobody. Just a customer. They bought a bunch of orders," Holly said, veiling the truth. She meant to tell Ro about the meeting with Oliver. But with everything going on she didn't have a chance. Now that it had been over a week she felt weird bringing it up. And so she just decided to omit the truth.

❄

It was dark out by the time Holly got home. The fair was over. Her whole body ached and if she heard sleigh bells one more time she would be dreaming about it for the next six months. They had sold out of bouquets completely and only had one box left of the cookies. Ro had gone to her parent's home to drop off the box of cookies for her parents and brothers.

Holly had crunched the numbers on the point of sales system. She would just about make it. It was more than they had sold in the entire last quarter.

They had done it. She would have enough money for the repairs and for the engineer. Holly let out a sigh as she flopped onto a chair in the kitchen. She brought out her phone and sent an e-transfer right away to Christopher. She hadn't yet paid him. He had said that she could delay until after the holiday. But with the high of adrenaline she felt from the fair, she may as well send it now.

The house was quiet as she opened the door of the fridge. She brought out the carton of milk and poured herself a glass, which she chugged down. She poured another and drank that as well. When was the last time she had fluids in her? She set down the glass with a clink.

Holly sat down again.

The house was quiet. All she could hear in the house was the tick of the black cat cuckoo clock that Rowena had insisted they hang in the kitchen. She rubbed an arm up and down, trying to get the chill out from her bones.

Holly opened the fridge door. Ketchup. No. A slightly squishy apple. Nope. There was absolutely nothing in the fridge that looked good. There were just ingredients and nothing easy or simple for her to eat. She closed the door of the fridge, turning to the pantry.

She opened the door. There was flour, sugar, and an assortment of dried goods. She was starving and yet hungry for nothing. She settled on a granola bar.

She sat again as she opened the foil wrapper.

She opened her phone again. Scrolling through her email. There was junk mail a few order updates and a few bill notifications in there but not much else.

Her phone lit up.

Jack.

> (J) I hope the fair today went
> well.

The message hit her like a punch to the gut. He had done as she had asked him. This was the first message he had sent her since she had asked him to let her go. He had *let her go*. Her mother's voice had gotten in her head. Now that the store was safe, and she could afford to repair the building, it was settling in how hollow it felt.

She was relieved that she had enough money to dig herself out of the hole that she was stuck in. But at what cost? She had fallen for him and that scared the hell out of her. It was easier to lose him than it was for him to potentially realize that she wasn't worth it after all. She had used the distraction of the emergency with the store to distract her from the pain of separating herself from him. From pushing him away.

She had been wretched to him. She had taken Jack's goodwill and had thrown them in his face. Her eyes stung. She pinched the bridge of her nose to try to stop the tears that threatened to fall.

The front door opened and Ro came in and hung up her coat.

"The boys were thrilled by the extra cookies. I'm considering it part of my Christmas gift to them this year." She entered the kitchen and saw Holly sitting there. Her mouth hung open as she took in the sight of her best friend falling apart.

"What's wrong? What happened?"

A knock sounded at her bedroom door.

"Go away," Holly said, wrapping the blanket closer around herself. She closed her eyes tight. They were red and swollen from the tears that wouldn't stop coming. Holly didn't want to see the world. Not yet.

"No," said a masculine voice. When Holly opened her eyes she saw Jack standing in the doorway of her bedroom. She thought she spied Ro looking guilty and duckling behind the door before she could be acknowledged. But who else could have called Jack?

Jack entered her room. His frame filled the doorway. He closed the door behind him. "You look tired," She said, noting the dark skin beneath his eyes. Jack nodded. He was kind enough not to remark on her own appearance, which she knew was disheveled.

She was exhausted enough not to be embarrassed by the fact that she had put on the sweatshirt that she had borrowed at his cabin. She hadn't washed it, not wanting it to lose his scent that was ingrained in the fabric.

"Ro called me." Holly pulled her lips into a thin line. She

had assumed as much. She couldn't stop crying no matter what she had tried. Ro had comforted her as much as possible. But this was beyond even her own powers.

Jack slowly entered the room, as if she was a scared cat about to bolt if he moved too quickly. He sat down at the edge of her bed. Jack rubbed her back as she let the tears dampen her pillow. Holly opened the covers with an invitation. Jack bent down to untie his shoes before swinging his legs onto the bed and resting his back against the headboard.

"I'm sorry I was such a jerk," she said, whipping her nose with the sleeve of her pajama set, she rolled so that her head was leaning against his chest. He pulled her in close, wrapping his arms around her. She felt so safe and like the world was more manageable in his arms. Like everything was finally going to be okay.

"Everything with the shop just completely overwhelmed me. And I felt like I could only focus on one thing."

"You're holding yourself to an impossible standard," Jack said. "You'll never be able to hold yourself up to this pressure."

"It's okay to take a day off and prioritize you. You matter, Holly. Regardless of *if* or *how badly* you mess up."

"I can take care of myself." Holly sniffed, knowing that she sounded like a petulant child.

"I know you can. Of course, I know that you can. You're the strongest person I know. But I *want* to take care of you, Holly." He looked deeply into her eyes and she knew he was telling the truth.

Being taken care of, not being the one doing the caring was an unfamiliar thing to her. Her fingers tangled together with his. She felt safe with him. His thumb brushed over the palm of her hand and she buried her head in his chest, listening to his heartbeat.

"She knew about the leak. My mom did. Maybe yours too." Holly took a big breath in. "But she knew and she did nothing about it. She sacrificed everything for that shop. And yet she couldn't even take care of it when it needed her." She squeezed her eyes tight. In truth, she wasn't sure if she was talking about the shop, or if she was talking about herself. Her mom had sacrificed everything, even Holly's childhood in pursuit of flowers. In pursuit of something more than what she already had in front of her. And in many ways, Holly felt like she loved working more than she loved her.

"It's okay to be angry at your mom for letting you down," Jack said gently as if she was going to break.

Holly wanted to scream at him that she wasn't angry at her mom. But that wasn't true. And he saw right through her bullshit. She was furious at her mom. She was angry. So angry that it threatened to overwhelm her if she thought about it too much. So she kept it down. She kept it secret. She *couldn't* feel angry. For what kind of daughter would be angry at her saint of a mom? Her *dead* mom.

She felt like the anger she kept down deep inside was disrespectful to the memory of her mom. You were supposed to respect and be reverent of the dead. But here she was hating her mother for not being there for her when she needed her the most.

She loved her mother. She missed her mother with every fiber of her being. And there wasn't a day that she didn't think about her mother. But she felt like she was betrayed by her mother.

As an adult woman, she could see now that her mother fought with her own demons and she felt a great deal of empathy with the life her mother led. She had endured heartache and strife at the hands of her father. But the child in Holly was hurting. Her mother had kept a roof over her head and food on the table but emotionally, Holly had to be the adult in that relationship. She was the one who took care of her mother when she fell apart.

Holly looked into Jack's eyes. *He would take care of her.* The concept felt foreign to her. He had made that promise when they were children. He had been so patient with her. So kind to her. But she didn't know if she was ready to let him in. For if she let him in she might get hurt again.

She had messed things up with them. Badly.

"Then I went and made things weird between us." Holly broke his gaze and played with the strings of the hoodie she was wearing.

"No, I'm sorry. I made the mistake. I shouldn't have let things get so far without thinking of the consequences."

"A mistake," Holly repeated, toying with the word on her tongue. Their time at the cabin hadn't *felt* like a mistake.

"I can't *not* have you in my life. I can't bear it or endure it. I'm not strong enough to have you not be in it. Can we just go back to what it was before?" *Before*. Holly's heart froze like time had stopped. She didn't know if she could go back to what it was before. Or if she wanted to go back. But she knew she wanted Jack in her life, in whatever way that made sense. She knew that she had feelings for him. Deep feelings that tied her heart to his and it ached at the thought of not being able to be close to him. But she knew that she was broken in many ways too. And she had to find a way to heal herself before giving herself to another. She had to find happiness in her.

"Sure," she said, "friends." He brushed a hand down her arm. And she snuggled into his chest. Cuddling wasn't exactly what *friends* did, but he didn't seem to be moving an inch to let her go, and she wasn't exactly going to move either. She enjoyed the closeness she felt with them and wondered if their friendship could truly get through this as just friends.

SIX DAYS UNTIL CHRISTMAS

❄

*H*olly woke up warm. Her pillow was unusually hard. A heavy arm was draped over her midsection. She looked up to see Jack looking down at her. How long had he been up? They had fallen asleep in her bedroom. Holly stretched her arms out. It was the best sleep she had gotten in days. Deep and restful.

"Morning," she said, making sure to wipe the drool that had collected at the side of her mouth.

"Morning." The corners of his eyes crinkled, but Holly could sense some reservation in his smile. Jack removed his arm as she woke and Holly's heart ached in its absence.

She tried to school her face into an impassive expression. She wasn't sure how they could go back to how things were before. Especially as she remembered the feelings of his hands on her body. Her core heated as she remembered their time in the cabin. Moments that had been haunting her dreams daily. Holly's eyes flicked down to Jack's lips. She flicked her tongue to wet her own.

Jack searched her eyes and his gaze darkened. Her gaze lingered on his lips. Her body was suddenly attuned to every inch that their bodies were touching. Holly sucked in a quick breath.

"Okay," she said, removing herself from the bed. She had to remove herself from the situation before she was tempted to ruin things *again*.

"Right," Jack said slowly, bringing a hand to rake through his hair. Jake sat up and Holly looked him over. He was still fully clothed in the clothing he was wearing yesterday, his jeans included. She felt a little awkward that she hadn't thought to find him something to wear to bed. Not that she had planned for him to stay over. She hadn't. She had just fallen asleep in his arms and the next thing she knew it was morning.

Holly felt an awkwardness fall over her. How was she supposed to act with Jack now? *Friends*. She repeated the word in her mind.

They had been just friends for so long. As long as she could remember really. But now the word now felt strange on her tongue.

Jack shifted on his feet.

"I should go," he said, but he didn't move. As if his feet were betraying him.

"You should go," Holly repeated. She took an unconscious step forward as if her feet were betraying her. Jack's gaze raked over her. Their eyes met. The way he looked at her now would be enough to make anyone blush. As if he was replaying every moment they shared together in the cabin in his head.

"Or I could stay." Holly didn't realize that she was nodding. Jack took a step forward. His form close enough that she could feel the warmth from his body. Her breath quickened as she looked up at him. A warmth spread through her as his hand came up to her chin. A thumb brushed against her jawline.

Jack took a deep breath in before stepping past her.

"I'll get us coffee," he said as if shaking something off.

Holly nodded slowly in disappointment as Jack walked to her bedroom door. He paused with his hand grasping the doorknob. She thought for a moment that he might turn back. But Jack straightened, opened the door, and walked through, closing the door behind him.

❄

"Holy shit," Holly said, sitting up straight, as she stared at an email on her laptop. She didn't want to blink in case the email would disappear if she took her eyes off of it. Her legs had been tangled in Jack's who was lying on the couch opposite her.

"What?" he said, looking up from a book. Jack had come back with coffees and pastry from the cafe down the road. They had spent the day talking and lazing around, trying to get back to some semblance of normality.

"I just got an order request in. It's for fifty thousand dollars."

"Holy shit," Jack repeated, sitting up on the couch.

"It's for three days from now," she said, deflating. "There's no way I can get enough flowers in that short period of time."

"If only you knew a flower farm with lots of flowers ready to go," Jack said absentmindedly, turning a page of his book.

Holly looked up at Jack slowly. A small smile crept over his face, his eyes fixated back on his book.

"What?" he asked, not looking up.

"I would pay you. No, credit you." She jumped on him with a hug. Jack let out a puff of air as she landed on him. "I'd love you forever." The words slipped out of her before she knew what she was saying.

Jack froze. Holly felt her ears go red hot.

"I would owe you so much." She breathed out, pretending that she hadn't said anything about love. She released him from her hug, pushing herself up. She turned back to the computer.

"It would be nothing." Jack coughed and looked at the ceiling.

She sent off a quick text message to Mia and Finley.

"No. Not nothing." Jack looked down at her, sitting next to him. She could feel his gaze on her. She paused for a moment. Her fingers hovered over the keys. Holly breathed in as she turned her face towards him. He was so close their noses could have touched.

Holly looked up at him from under her lashes. Her breath hitched as she moved an inch closer. Holly could smell his aftershave. Their noses touched and Holly closed her eyes.

"I ordered Chinese food." Ro came into the room, carrying a large bowl of popcorn.

Holly and Jack whipped apart. Holly's opened her eyes wide and Jack let out a puff of breath. Holly could feel him clench and unclench his hand beside her. Ro narrowed her eyes at the two of them, looking between them.

Holly turned her laptop towards Ro before she could say anything. Ro's eyes widened.

"That's a lot of zeros," Ro said, inspecting the email. "Is that the ball you were invited to?"

"Yeah," Holly said, her heart started to beat faster. She couldn't keep it to herself any longer. She didn't want to either.

"I've been keeping a secret." She heard her heartbeat in her ears, thunderingly loud. "I've been meeting with this guy. Met. Actually. It only happened once." Holly stumbled over her words.

"He's an investor from the Ridgemont Investor Company,

the one that has been developing property on Main Street. He stopped in the flower shop a few months back to give me his card and I had a meeting with him a few days ago. He stopped by at the fair." Holly squeezed her eyes tight and waited for the yelling to begin. She had kept this a secret for the past month from the two people in the world that she didn't keep secrets from.

She peaked one eye open. Jack and Ro shared a look between themselves before looking at Holly. They waited patiently for a moment as if expecting her to say more or to reveal something else.

"That's it?" Ro deadpanned, she dropped her arms down, which were still holding the large bowl of popcorn.

"Hol, I thought you were going to tell us that you were pregnant with his baby or something like that. Meeting with an investor isn't exactly a big secret. I'm pretty sure half the business owners in town have met with them at one point or another."

"Another point in Mrs. Greywell's bad books." Holly elbowed him in the ribs. Jack coughed.

"I've got to go to the shop. I've got to pick up supplies." Holly stood.

"Holly. It's six in the evening. It's Cole River. Everything is closed," Ro said slowly, her eyebrows raised.

Holly deflated. But Ro was right. Everything would be closed at this time. Unless she wanted to drive into the city. Holly peeked outside. Snowing again. No. She would not be driving to the city at this hour. It was already dark outside and she hated driving in the dark. She could make some orders online.

"Plus, we have Chinese food coming." Ro sat on the ground, placing the popcorn on the coffee table and crossing her legs. She grabbed the television remote and turned it on, flipping through the movies available to stream.

"Are we feeling swords and sandals or film noir?" Ro asked.

Holly gave a noise of indifference as she penned an email to respond to Marla and Oliver that she was able to complete the order. Although Oliver had included a lot of the details that she would need for the order, she attached a form that she typically sent to clients, as well as requested a phone meeting as soon as possible. Jack and Rowena were bickering over what movie to put on as Holly sent out the email. She let out a sigh. She looked at her two friends.

Ro kept scrolling through movies and Jack shaking his head. She wouldn't be surprised if an all out brawl didn't start if they didn't agree on a movie soon. As they were distracted, Holly pulled up the Ridgemont Investment Company website. She scrolled through, clicking a few links on the site before scrolling over to the *About Us* section. The website was filled with the typical nonsense buzzwords and vague language, but there, with her hands confidently placed at her sides, was a headshot of Marla Fairfax. The CEO. Even though the woman was smiling, she looked just as intimidating in the photo as she did in real life.

"Fairfax?" Ro said, as she pressed play on the remote and sat next to Holly on the couch. After much argument, they had decided on *River of No Return*, a classic country movie that the three of them had watched many times before. Too many times. *River of No Return* was like Switzerland for the two of them. Neutral ground.

"Yeah." Holly looked at Ro. "Do you know of her?" Holly felt her body tense. Maybe Ro had heard some horrible tale of Marla Fairfax. Maybe she was the big bad wolf and Holly was the sheep ready to be slaughtered.

"Any relation to Preston Fairfax? They're one of the oldest and wealthiest families in town. He used to do business with my mum." Holly's eyes rose. Rowena's mum, though retired now, was the foremost well known architect in town. Much of the west coast really. She had gained some notoriety for her design in the late eighties and then moved into consulting after that. People from all over the country would come to do business with her.

How had she never heard of the Fairfax family name before?

"My brothers used to tell me some rumor that they had gotten their wealth from piracy back in the day and had settled in Cole River to live out their days in peace after they gave up life as scallywags." Ro made a hook with a finger and gave her best pirate impression a go.

"But mum never gave credence to the tale."

Holly pulled up a flower supply company onto her computer browser. She would be able to purchase all of the basics that she would need without confirming the details with the client. She needed them to call her. She checked her watch to double check that she hadn't missed a call. Nothing.

Ro pushed the lid of her laptop down slowly and pulled it out of her arms. 'No working,' she mouthed as she replaced the laptop with the bowl of popcorn. Holly rolled her eyes as the actor Robert Mitchum appeared on the screen chopping down a tree before wandering rugged mountainside. Holly let herself get lost in the opening song, letting a feeling of familiarity and nostalgia wash over her.

"I'll go with you," Jack said, nudging her. Holly looked up to see Jack smiling sheepishly at her. "If you're looking for a date."

Ro made a shushing noise, grabbing a fist full of popcorn and popping it in her mouth.

Jack looked Holly in the eye. Her gaze softened. She had planned to ask him. If he was inclined to go, but she had been afraid that it wouldn't be his scene.

"Will you? It'll probably be stupidly fancy. You'll have to wear a suit and—"

"Sounds like fun," he said, giving her a reassuring squeeze. She knew for a fact that this was not his type of fun. But he wanted to go for her nonetheless, and that mattered.

"Thank you," Holly said.

THREE DAYS UNTIL CHRISTMAS

❄

"*T*here should be a reservation under Holly MacIntosh." Holly fiddled with her phone, tapping it on the front counter of the hotel.

"Yes, I see you right here. For two guests." Holly nodded. The woman at the front counter looked behind Holly briefly, looking for the second guest. Jack had said that he would meet her at the hotel later in the day.

"My friend will be here shortly. I can check in without him, right?" Holly hadn't stayed at many hotels, barely any as an adult at least, and the process always stressed her out. This hotel in particular was somewhere she could never have afforded to stay. She could tell from the marble and polished wood detailing that covered every surface of the hotel.

"Of course," The woman said, her long fingernails making a loud tapping noise as she entered their details into the computer. She slid her chair over to the far side of the counter. She grabbed two plastic cards and slid them into a little paper pouch before passing them to Holly.

"You're in room 2412. The penthouse had a separate keyed access, so you'll need to swipe your key in the elevator." The woman gestured to the right where the room opened up to a grand staircase that split into two separate entrances, merging back at the top at a balcony that overlooked the lobby.

"Penthouse," Holly repeated. "There has to be a mistake."

The woman's brow furrowed for a moment as she looked back at the computer.

"No mistake, ma'am. Your reservation is under the penthouse suite. The bellboy at the bottom of the stairs will take your bags. I hope you enjoy your time here." The woman gave her a polite smile, but Holly could tell she was confused as much as Holly was. Holly certainly didn't look the type to have rented a penthouse suite.

Holly turned back to the woman.

"Can I leave a key here for my friend?" The woman nodded, taking down his information and placing the key that Holly passed back under the desk. Holly took a deep breath before grabbing the handle of her suitcase and rolling it toward the stairs. Holly was almost embarrassed as she handed over her suitcase, which had seen better days. It was an embroidered floral fabric, the kind you would see on old couches or old women's handbags. She had inherited it from her mother, who she was pretty sure had inherited it from her mother. It was fraying at the edges. But the wheels were metal and the handle mechanism was metal and it had stood the tests of time, and Holly couldn't justify the cost of getting new luggage for the few times she left town.

She checked her watch as she stepped up the stairs. Mia had just texted her that the set-up at the venue was about halfway done and that Jack and Bernard had just arrived with the second delivery of their stock and that Jack was on his way over to her. They had all come into town early that morning to set up. She was thankful for her staff that she

162 | ALEX GILLIE

could trust them to finish the set-up while she was away from the venue to get ready for the event.

She had half felt like saying she wasn't going and to just stay at the venue and to finish the set-up but Jack had reassured her that they had everything under control. He would join her after an hour, which would give her time to get her hair done at the salon in the hotel lobby.

Mia had practically pushed Holly out of the venue so she would have time to get ready for the event. Holly and Jack would return to the venue early to ensure that everything was ready and absolutely perfect for when the event started.

An event like this was a massive opportunity for her company to gain future business. From the grandeur she had already experienced and by the size and some of the names she had read on the place cards while putting together the centerpieces, there were some very powerful people in attendance at tonight's event.

Holly came to two large elevator doors. A man in a red uniform greeted her as she stepped inside and asked for her room number. He had pressed the button and asked that she swipe her card at a little black portal located in the elevator wall.

Holly tapped the card against the palm of her hand as the elevator went up and up. It felt like an eternity as she watched a golden hand go past each floor in a mechanism at the top of the elevator door. Finally, with the ring of a bell, the elevator doors opened to a small culvert with a single door at the end. The walls were lined with a velvet patterned wallpaper. She stepped out of the elevator as the man gave her a small bow of his head. The doors closed behind her.

She approached the door, swiping her key yet again, and reached for the handle.

The door opened up into a long foyer with several other entrances on each of the walls. Holly's mouth hung open.

This wasn't a hotel room. It was practically a whole house. And it seemed larger than her own. The walls were paneled in a creamy white and lit with the most stunning warm crystal sconces.

Holly walked down to the first entrance, which was marked by two french doors. She had to be careful not to get lost in here. She pondered for a moment if she shouldn't leave a trail of breadcrumbs lest she lost her way. She slid open the doors which opened up into a full on living room with the most plush looking couches she had ever seen. Wall to wall windows showed the splendor of the city lit during the Christmas season. The city sparkled. She stood there for a moment, taking it all in.

Holly didn't want to think about what a hotel room like this cost per night. Thankfully she wasn't the one paying the bill. Marla had her assistant send over the reservation along in one of the many emails she had been sending back and forth in the past few days about the event. Holly closed her eyes. A few days ago she was in a very different place than she was now. It seemed like everything was finally fitting in place. But Holly had this sinking feeling of waiting for the other shoe to drop.

Holly's watch buzzed. She scrolled to see the final photos of the venue that Mia had sent. Everything looked perfect. Just like she had envisioned it. She blew out a breath of relief and tried to relax her body. Holly shrugged off her coat and placed it on the back of the couch. She spotted a bottle of champagne and a card that had been placed on the coffee table.

Holly picked up the card and turned it over. In large cursive letters, the card spelled out a single word. *Congratulations*.

The room opened up to a full dining room with a large oval table with six matching chairs seated around it. A crystal chandelier was hung above that cast a beautiful shadow across the room.

Holly went back to the entrance and peeked in the other room. It was a full office with a stately looking desk in the middle made of polished mahogany wood. She turned back and opened the final door.

The room was massive. It was larger than any bedroom she had ever seen. Curtains that rippled in very satisfying symmetry hung on the wall along with elegant oil paintings of still life fruit and flowers. *How fitting.*

A king bed was positioned perfectly in the middle of the room. Holly felt the fabric beneath her hands. Soft as silk, yet crisp as cotton. *One bed.*

"I guess I'll sleep on the couch." Holly whipped her head over to the entrance where Jack stood, a crooked smile on his face. He was leaning against the frame of the door with a suit bag hanging over one of his shoulders.

Holly pulled in her lips.

"I can ask that they change our rooms?" Holly raised her eyebrow at him, giving him a small smile.

"Absolutely not." Jack let out a laugh. He placed his suit on a chair in the corner of the room before grabbing Holly's hand and leading her to the window. "I'm not giving up this view."

The room opened up to a large balcony that looked as if it had heated seating based on the distinct lack of snow she noticed on the balcony. This high up, they were seated with the skyscrapers. Tall pillars that dotted the landscape of the downtown. Glittering as the glass reflected light all around.

"You deserve this. Especially with all of the work you've put in the last few days," Jack said, coming behind her and wrapping his arms around her. She leaned into him.

They weren't very good at being just friends it seemed. They couldn't seem to be able to keep away from each other.

A little touch here, a brush there. She could tell that her staff had noticed the change in them.

Even with the stress of the event tonight, Holly felt lighter than she had in months. Jack had stayed over the past few nights. Holly had gotten used to using Jack as a pillow. Ro hadn't even said a word, she had just accepted Jack as a new roommate and had added his name to the chore chart one morning.

Jack rested his head on the top of hers as they swayed for a moment, content in each other's company.

"Don't you have a hair appointment?" Jack said. Holly glanced down at her watch.

"Shit."

❄

Holly looked at herself in the mirror hung on the wall of the hotel room. She used her hands to brush down the silk of the dress. The fabric was a blue as deep as the midnight sky on a new moon. It hugged her upper body but flowed outward as it reached her hips. Small crystals were pressed into the dress at the bodice in the shape of starbursts and shot out like shooting stars down the skirt. She pressed her fingers to the neckline that cut her straight across the shoulders. The dress came tightly down her arms to a point at her wrists. It felt like a second skin.

She had bought this dress a few years ago when she was still with Benji. It was one of the items she kept when she and Benji had broken up. She had bought it one day when she was out in the City. She had bought it for the galas she used to go to for his work, and although she tried it on every time there was an event, she always ended up putting it back in its box and she wore something else. This dress felt too personal. To *her* to wear to one of

Benji's events. Like she was exposing a raw part of herself to the world. So instead she would put it back to wear something more in line with the Holly that Benji had expected of her.

But she didn't want to hide herself any longer. Jack was right. She *thought* that she had been prioritizing herself, but she was hiding in somebody else's dreams, not her own. She had hid in the persona that she thought Benji had wanted of her, in his dreams, then she had hid in her mother's. But she didn't want to hide any longer. She wanted to let herself show to the world.

Holly had gone to the salon in the hotel to have her hair done, it was pinned into an updo, simple, yet Holly knew she could never recreate it without help. The stylist had put some kind of finishing oil in her hair that made her hair glisten like spun gold. She knew she would have to go purchase some before leaving the city.

She looked at herself in the mirror. Really looked at herself. She stood a little taller. She took a deep breath in.

Jack came out of the bathroom where he was getting ready.

"Wow." Jack stopped in his tracks, his gaze lingering on her form.

"You are so beautiful." He breathed out a breath.

Holly blushed.

"You don't look so bad yourself." Jack was wearing a simple but well tailored tuxedo. The tuxedo was made of a matte black material with a single satin ribbon running down the leg of the pants. He adjusted the links on his cuff, made of mother of pearl. He looked as handsome as ever. Not a single strand of his devilish blonde hair was out of place.

"After you," Jack said, swinging an arm out to beckon Holly out the door.

❄

Everything looked perfect. Mia and Finley had finished the set-up. They had completed the instructions that Holly had left behind to a tee and had headed back to Cole River with the truck and extra supplies.

Holly surveyed the scene. Most of the guests had arrived by now. Everybody looked splendid. The venue looked splendid. The atmosphere was splendid. A band played in the corner of the room with a woman in a long black dress sang a blues song. Her voice was smooth like butter.

The guests mingled at tables, each had a tall metal frame that held up large flowing arrangements filled with dark green foliage and pure white blooms. The tables centered around a circular table that held a tall arrangement that shot up to the ceiling. Flowers and foliage and twigs that twirled and twisted out like shooting stars. A single spotlight hit the arrangement, making it look like a piece in an art gallery. At the entrance of the room where guests arrived as well as the podium at the front of the room were two matching arches, so packed with florals that it looked like a rosebush had grown out of the floor and had climbed the wall to make an arch. Finally, hanging from invisible thread, there were rosebuds and petals hanging from the ceiling all throughout the room, making it look like it was snowing flowers.

With such a large budget, Holly was able to accomplish a design she had only dreamed of. She breathed out a sigh of relief that everything had gone off without a hitch. Holly looked up, admiring her design as she was approached by Marla. Marla was wearing a sleek red dress that fell off the shoulder with a small train that flowed elegantly from the back. She held a matching clutch.

"Very impressive," Marla said, peering at Holly with a shrew look of approval.

"Thank you," Holly said with a smile.

"I knew you wouldn't disappoint me."

Jack came up behind her, placing a hand on the small of her back and placing a glass of champagne in her hand.

"And who is this?" Marla asked, looking at Jack up and down. Marla gave Jack the same look that Holly imagined she would give a large wad of cash.

"This is my—" Holly paused for a moment. What was Jack to her? The lines had blurred and she wasn't quite sure what label to give him. "This is... Jack." She settled on just *Jack*.

Marla looked between the two of them.

"Oh, I see," she said, winking at Holly.

"I hope you do consider our offer." Holly shifted on her feet. Marla smiled at her but didn't wait for an answer, but excused herself with a wave and walked to greet another guest who caught her eye.

"She didn't look much like a pirate," Jack whispered in her ear. Holly elbowed him in the ribs. Jack let out a puff of air.

"You're surprisingly strong for somebody so small," He said, rubbing the area she had jabbed. Jack twirled her in his arms so she was looking at him.

"Are you?" Holly asked, looking Jack in the eye. Jack's smile was wiped from his face.

"Am I what?" He asked, looking nervous.

"*Just* Jack to me?" Holly searched his eyes. Jack had said that he wanted to go back to what they were before. That everything had been a mistake between them. But his actions since then told her differently. Holly thought that she could wait for things to figure themselves out. For *her* to figure herself out. But she realized that she didn't want to do it alone.

She realized that she could rely on Jack for support and she also *wanted* to. She wanted to share her life with him. The good things and the bad. But she needed to know if he did as well.

Jack brought a hand up to tuck a stray strand of hair behind her ear. He paused before saying, "I'm whatever you want me to be."

"I love you, Jack Stirling," Holly said as she looked into his eyes. There. She had said it, without regret or hesitation.

Jack froze. Shock was clear on his face. Like he wasn't even breathing.

"I love you," she repeated, her eyebrows scrunched in the middle. "And I think I've loved you for a very long time," Holly said, looking deep into his eyes, confident in what she was saying and what she wanted. She wanted him.

"I don't want to keep doing this. I don't want to keep pretending like the cabin didn't happen. Like *we* didn't happen."

Jack leaned down and captured her lips in his. The kiss was sweet and chaste.

A song played in the ballroom and Holly immediately recognized it as the same jazz song that they had danced to at the cabin that night before everything went to shit. Her heart fluttered, squeezing and clenching. She could feel every heartbeat as it rang in her ears.

He gave her one of his best smiles. Her heart skipped a beat. Jack offered a hand out to Holly, bowing slightly. Holly grinned back at him. She put down her glass of champagne on a round crystal table.

Jack placed one hand in hers and he led her to the middle of the dance floor. The room was dimly lit, and as they danced it seemed like the remainder of the guests disappeared and it was only them again. Like they had been at the cabin. Jack expertly moved them about the room and Holly let him lead her. She didn't need to think as he twirled her around.

"I think I'm going to sell the shop, Jack," Holly confessed. Jack's eyes widened, his eyes searching her face.

"At least the land that it's on."

She gave him a smile. Then placed her head on his chest.

"I never really wanted to deal with the hassle of being a property owner anyways. I was never good at it. I just wanted to sell flowers. That was the deal that Marla was talking about." Jack was silent as they moved across the dance floor.

"They're going to develop the land, tear down the building, but keep the facade. I found out through those old records that Christopher, the engineer, sent me that the front of the building is the only thing that is original anyways. The rest of it had burned in a fire in the fifties, leaving most of the building a reconstruction." She looked up at him from where she had been resting her head on his chest.

Holly was afraid for a moment that he would be disappointed in her for giving up. For selling to the investment company that the whole town seemed to be against. She was selling the place they had grown up in. The place that held so very many memories for both of them. But she was confident in her decision.

Jack looked down at her with nothing but understanding in his eyes and she knew without words that he supported her decision. He brought a single hand up to cup her face.

He tipped her chin up and kissed her. Jack rested his nose against hers as they swayed as the next song came on.

"Old Lady Greywell is going to be so mad," Jack said in her ear.

"Old Lady Greywell can eat me," Holly said back, scrunching up her nose.

"That's the spirit, MacIntosh," Jack responded.

"Let me grab our coats and let's get out of here." Holly nodded with a big grin. The event was far from over. But the speeches had concluded and all that was left was more dancing and an open bar. Jack crossed the room too where the coat check was.

Holly looked up to recognize a man who was standing on the opposite side. He was an older gentleman wearing a suit that was too big for him and he was standing next to a slender brunette woman who resembled a stork.

"Dad?"

❋

Her father didn't look up at hearing her voice. Having his daughter be here must be so far from his realm of possibility. Holly walked over to the man. Herschel MacIntosh. The man she got her name from.

"Dad," she repeated as she got closer. Still nothing. He gave out a bark of a laugh as if what was just said was the funniest thing he had ever heard.

"Hershel." She said his name instead, hoping that would finally catch his attention.

The man looked like he was about to wave her off as if she was a fly that had landed on him before his eyes widened with surprise and recognition.

"Holly? If you'll excuse me." He said to the group of men he was talking to and pulled her to one side.

"What are you doing here?" He asked in a hushed tone as if she was a child again who had wandered into a meeting with some of his important clients. Holly had heard the tone before.

"I was invited." She said plainly. Herschel looked at her with a confused expression on his face, as if not comprehending how his daughter could have possibly garnered an invitation.

The woman beside him looked at him expectantly, she looped her arm in his.

"Won't you introduce me to your friend?" The woman drawled, crawling two fingers up his arm.

"I'm his daughter," Holly said Holly looked down in disgust as she circled a finger on his chest. Holly stepped back as if being burned. The ring on the woman's finger looked familiar, too familiar It was her mother's ring.

Holly almost wanted to laugh if it wasn't so painful. This wasn't the woman that he had left her mother for. It wasn't even the second woman after that. Herschel had used the same ring for all of his wives. His numerous wives.

"Are you somebody's guest?" Herschel continued as if the woman hadn't interrupted. Jack, as if on cue, appeared by her side wearing his long black coat and had hers draped over his arm. Herschel nodded as if that must be it.

"No, Dad, I was invited. Me. You may not believe it but I am a guest of honor."

"How could you have been invited? This is an event for important people. Successful people. Not small town flower girls. Did you come here to get my attention?" Herschel said harshly, his eyes narrowed as if he had figured it out. Her cheeks flared red. And suddenly Holly felt like a little girl again, who had made a flower crown out of dandelions only for her father to have told her that dandelions were weeds and that her crown was disgusting.

"Dad, could you just not? How could I have known you would have been here? I was invited as a guest. My store--"

"You're just so sensitive," Holly's father said. "Just like your mother. She should have closed that business years ago. Especially with it bleeding all of that money. It was a money pit then and it's a money pit now." Her father said it as if it was a matter of fact. As if he was telling an old buddy about a bad stock to buy. Not his daughter. All of the blood rushed to Holly's head.

Jack stiffened beside her. Going dangerously still as he heard her father's biting words about his daughter. She squeezed his hand.

"Your daughter is amazing. Not that you would know that." Jack bit the words out. His hand clenched. Herschel's eyes widened in recognition of who Jack was.

"Is that how you talk to your elders, boy?" Herschel looked down at his nose at Jack. In her childhood, Holly saw her father as the biggest man that ever was, but now, standing in front of Jack her father looked small.

"Everything you see here. Is your daughter's work. She is talented, loyal to her friends, and is the most hard-working person you'll ever meet. She had persevered through so much and you can't even bother to be nice." Jack was seething. He bit out the words and Hershel at least had the decency to look embarrassed.

Holly put an arm on Jack, letting him know that she was okay. She didn't need protection. Not from *him*. Holly stood a little taller, holding her head up high.

"I am successful at what I do," Holly said, her voice clear. "And mom was successful in what she did. Without you, she thrived in her work. She was spectacular after you left. She won awards and catered to large events. Big ones. And was given a recognition that you never saw. And she taught me so much about the trade, not *you*. You were never there. And then when she was gone, where were you?"

"You could have reached out at any time," Herschel said, his hands crossing over his chest defensively.

"*You* were my parent. That was *your* job." Holly wanted to scream but she was proud that her voice held steady and calm.

"You were supposed to be there for me in my time of

need. To assure me that I was enough. That I was *good* enough. That you *loved* me. But instead, you confirmed the opposite."

Holly looked her nose down at him.

"I don't even think you know how to love," she said and he looked smaller than ever. He was no longer the man she so desperately wanted the love, affection, and attention of. She knew this now. It took her too long to see it. But she saw it now. She understood how a parent was meant to be with a child. She saw it through how she saw Jack with the triplets.

She knew that she was enough. Just as she was now.

She didn't need to change anything. And she didn't need validation from the man in front of her. The man who was her father in nothing but name.

Hershel opened and closed his mouth a few times. He looked so much smaller to her as she looked at him. Holly now saw him for what he was. A man. A small man. He just stood there dumbfounded and she couldn't tell if she saw even an ounce of remorse in his face.

She sucked in a breath and looked him in the eye.

"I forgive you," she said, and she meant it. He had never once apologized for how he treated her during her childhood and during the months after her mother's death. And she didn't even know if he recognized the hurt that he caused her. But that didn't matter. She would let go of the hurt, not for him. But for her. She had to.

It was a poison in her life. A wretched wound that wouldn't close.

The woman, who was his wife, looked between the two of them with a pained expression on her face. This was not the woman who her father had left her mother for. This was wife three or maybe four. Holly had lost track and hadn't cared to know their names or hold her hopes up for some sort of relationship. But this woman seemed nice enough to at least recognize that there was some strained relationship between this man and his child.

"I hope for happiness in your life. But I do not want to be a part of it." She had finally said it to him. A relief swept over her like a weighted blanket had been lifted off of her.

Holly didn't want to hear his response. Holly turned and left. Jack was moments behind her. He put a gentle hand on the small of her back.

"You okay?" Jack asked quietly so that only Holly could hear as they reached the front of the hotel. Holly nodded.

❄

Holly leaned against the door to the Hotel. She felt exhausted. Exhilarated. Confident. But exhausted. She swung her arms around Jack, stuffing her head in his neck.

"Thank you" she muttered into him.

"Your dad is an ass. As much of an ass as I remember him being," he said, hugging her closer.

Holly nodded in agreement.

"I meant everything I said," Jack said as Holly pulled away from him to look him in the eyes. Jack kissed her. She pushed into him, pressing her body against his. She wanted to feel him on her in every place possible. Jack returned the fervor, picking her up. Holly's legs came to wrap around his waist.

Jack broke the kiss, leaning his nose against hers. They breathed heavily together. Their chests rise and fall in sync with each other. He looked into her eyes.

"I love you, Holly MacIntosh. I have loved you since I can remember. Never faltering. Never failing. I will always love you."

ZERO DAYS UNTIL CHRISTMAS

❄

*T*he Stirling house was lit with candles, Christmas lights, and the soft glow of the fireplace. The air smelled like oranges and cinnamon sticks. Holly took a deep breath in as she entered the home, followed by Jack.

This was the first year that Holly joined the Stirlings for Christmas. Jack had asked her to join and for the first time, she had said yes. But now, entering the home with Christmas music playing from the other room, Holly felt nervous.

They entered the living room, which was decorated from top to bottom with baubles and garlands and nutcrackers. An older man, who Holly recognized as Jack's grandfather, sat in the corner with a pipe and a large newspaper open in front of him.

Paulette and Ralph were sitting by the fire. Ralph had a blanket wrapped around his wife and he was humming along to the Christmas song as he rocked them both back and forth.

The man was so obviously besotted with his wife. Holly looked at them and wondered how she had never noticed how obviously in love they were with each other. A small pang of jealousy for the childhood Jack had with very much in love parents hit her. She pushed the feeling down, as Paulette's eyes lit up as she saw Holly and Jack standing at the threshold to the living room.

"I'm so glad you could come," Paulette said as she got up from her spot by the fire and crossed the room to greet them. Holly nodded. Ralph gave a wave to the two of them from where he was seated. Holly gave a little wave back.

"Oh and you two, another little surprise." Paulette squeezed Holly's arm.

"I had almost given up on the prospect of grandchildren."

"Mom," Jack warned, giving her a look.

"I always knew you two would make a great couple if you wanted to be. I had hoped, at least. He's loved you forever, you know." Tears started to form in Paulette's eyes as she brought Holly in for a hug. Holly brought her hands up around her back. After a moment, Paulette released Holly, giving her another squeeze.

"Okay Mom, we're gonna go over here now," Jack said, waving his mother off and guiding Holly to a table that had an assortment of snacks.

"I'm going to go get drinks. Do you want a drink? I think I need a drink," Jack said, bringing a hand up to pinch his nose.

"Your mom is sweet. A drink would be nice," Holly said, giving him a quick peck on the cheek. Jack let out a sigh as he went around the table to the bar.

"I found the pickle," came a shout from behind the Christmas tree and the triplets emerged from behind it. Backaleigh was waving around a glass pickle ornament in her hands. The two boys had a scowl on their faces. A large smile spread across Beckaleigh's face as she saw Jack and Holly. Jack let out a huff of air as the two boys tackled him in a hug. They let out giggles as Jack picked up the two boys with a single swoop. He swung them around, tossing them both on the couch. The boys launched themselves at him again.

Holly smiled at them as Beckaleigh presented the pickle ornament to her.

"A pickle. How wonderful?" She said, indulging the girl, but not quite understanding the hype around a pickle. Other than pickles were delicious. But this pickle didn't look like one you could eat.

"The person who finds the pickle gets an extra present," said a woman's voice and Holly jumped a little, not expecting somebody to be beside her.

"Hi, I'm Beverly. You must be Holly. I've heard so much about you from my rambunctious gaggle of children." The woman held a hand out to her. She was not what Holly had expected. She was a little older than Jack and Holly, but she had a wise, almost librarian look about her. Holly shook her outreached hand.

"Very nice to meet you," Holly said. The woman could not have been more different than the woman who she had seen with her father. Holly realized that she had let her experiences judge the woman without meeting her. She had expected Beverly to be some woman who was only there to take advantage of an old man's money.

The triplets all came to wrap their hands around Beverly. She stooped down to give them all a large hug.

"My gaggle." She gave an exaggerated cry and started to shower all three in kisses. The kids all gave out giggles as they tried to wriggle out of their mother's arms.

"No fair. That's my pickle." Beckaleigh cried as Kayle grabbed it out of her hands.

"Finders keepers." He said, sticking out his tongue and holding the pickle just out of her reach

"Children," Their mother said, placing her hands on her hips. The woman turned to Holly.

"Excuse me while I deal with this dispute." The woman plucked the pickle out of the boy's hand and disappeared into the hall. The children followed her, bickering the whole way.

Jack came back with a small highball glass in hand. Jack nodded for Holly to follow him into the kitchen. He placed the glasses on the table, before searching the cupboards for a small flask.

"Eggnog," he said, pouring some of the liquid from the flask into each glass.

"With a bit of a spice," he said, tapping his nose.

Holly let out a laugh, taking the glass from Jack. She took a sip. The eggnog was delightfully cold, but a warmth filled her as it slid down her throat.

Holly gave a noise of approval, taking another sip.

"Merry Christmas, Jack." Holly passed a small present wrapped in a bright red metallic wrapping. The present made no noise as he shook it. An eyebrow raised.

Jack unwrapped the silk ribbon that tied a small card to the box and then carefully peeled back each edge of the wrapping paper, careful not to rip it. Inside, lay a leatherbound book with foiled letters and a gilded edge.

"Walden by David Henry Thoreau," Jack said to himself. He flipped the book over, feeling the leather beneath the pads of his fingers. Jack opened the book to a passage and read it out loud.

"*Live in each season as it passes; breathe the air, drink the drink, taste the fruit, and resign yourself to the influence of the earth.*" Jack closed the book, rubbing a thumb over the gold-foiled letters on the spine. He looked at Holly with wonder. His brow furrowed.

"Did you know that Waldon was one of my favorite books?"

Holly let out a small laugh. "It was a hunch." She tapped the side of her nose.

"And I saw a pretty worn out copy in your collection at the cabin." She stuck her tongue between her teeth. Jack put the book aside and kissed her hand.

Jack put the book down on the kitchen table and took out a small velvet satchel from behind his back pocket and gave it to Holly. "Merry Christmas, Hol." He said.

The bag was small enough to fit in the palm of her hand. Jack looked at her expectantly. She pressed the bag between her fingers. There was something hard inside. Holly inserted her two pointer fingers into the mouth of the bag and pulled it open. She turned the bag upside down and a little wooden ornament fell out. It was a whittled rose. Holly recognized it as the object that Jack was whittling the day they spent together in his cabin.

As Holly looked at Jack she realized that there were good people in this world and that this man– her best friend– was one of the best. Holly thought she knew everything about Jack. Turns out, she was just getting started. Jack noticed her looking at him and cocked his head. A small smile crept into his face.

"I love you, Jack Stirling." Holly tipped her head to kiss Jack, right there in the kitchen. He picked her up and spun her around, kissing her back. He placed her gently back on the ground, pressing his forehead to hers.

"I love you too, Holly Macintosh."

The End

ABOUT THE AUTHOR

Alex Gillie writes romance and fantasy novels. She is a loving wife and mother to one wonderful girl and another wonderful pup. Alex loves taking long summer walks through nature with her family, sipping hot cocoa on a cold winter day, and the smell of fresh snow.

In A Snowdrop Kiss is Alex Gillie's debut novel.

Alex's next book, *In a Wicked Kiss*, will be out in Summer 2025.

If you enjoyed this book, please consider leaving a review.

Follow to keep updated on upcoming releases.

Instagram: @AlexGillieAuthor

TikTok: @AlexGillieAuthor

42792248R00109